SIN

IS THE NEW

LOVE

MW00467230

SIN
IS THE NEW
LOVE

ABIR MUKHERJEE

Srishti
PUBLISHERS & DISTRIBUTORS

SRISHTI PUBLISHERS & DISTRIBUTORS
Registered Office: N-16, C.R. Park
New Delhi – 110 019
Corporate Office: 212A, Peacock Lane
Shahpur Jat, New Delhi – 110 049
editorial@srishtipublishers.com

First published by
Srishti Publishers & Distributors in 2018

Copyright © Abir Mukherjee, 2018

10 9 8 7 6 5 4 3 2 1

This is a work of fiction. The characters, places, organisations and events described in this book are either a work of the author's imagination or have been used fictitiously. Any resemblance to people, living or dead, places, events, communities or organisations is purely coincidental.

The author asserts the moral right to be identified as the author of this work.

All rights reserved. No part of this publication may be reproduced, stored in a retrieval system, or transmitted, in any form or by any means, electronic, mechanical, photocopying, recording or otherwise, without the prior written permission of the Publishers.

Printed and bound in India

Acknowledgments

I would like to thank my family for their continuous support in all phases of my life.

Thanks to Mr. J.K. Bose, Mr. Arup Bose and Srishti Publishers & Distributors for having faith in me and giving me the opportunity to be published under their esteemed publication house.

Thanks to my editors Lachmi Bose Deb Roy and Stuti. Without you, the following bunch of papers would not have got the shape of a book.

"I am sorry, *sona*. We were just scared of losing you forever," Ahi's mother mumbled, her quivering palms cupping Ahi's bloodstained face.

Ahi glanced at her mother blank-eyed, with no attempt of answering her, and pushed her hands away slowly before ambling towards the bathroom. Blood oozed through every single twill of her white top and was dripping onto her jeans. Her mother failed to keep herself strong, perceiving the numbness of her cheerful daughter.

"Don't worry, she is absolutely fine," Ahi's father consoled her vulnerable mother whose world revolved around her husband and daughter. She hid her face with the extended end of her saree and started weeping. He embraced her tightly, concealing his apprehension that this one incident could damage Ahi's psychology permanently and could destruct his perfect family forever.

Ahi pulled off her top, jeans and inner wear sluggishly and stood in front of the mirror like a mannequin with an expressionless face and still eyes brooding in the battle of contradictory thoughts in her mind. The unevenly scattered, dark-red blood looked more vivid on Ahi's milky-white skin. She rubbed the four fingers of her right hand under her breast where the blood had not coagulated till then and brushed her palm on her face, making a mask of blood. She leaned close to the mirror. Her breathing formed a drape of vapour on the mirror, blurring her reflection. That natural incident crushed her numbness. She started wiping the mirror like a kid, contorting her face. However, her bloody hand made the mirror dirtier. She screamed at the top of her voice in frustration and kneeled on the floor.

"Ahi, please open the door," her mother requested, weeping and thumping on the door. There was no response from inside other than a feeble sound of crying.

"Ahi, just talk to us," her father tried, a vain attempt.

Eventually, Ahi noticed that conch tattooed on her thigh, partly proclaiming its existence beneath the bloodstain. She had been hating that tattoo all the time since she had got the gumption of puberty, as it was not in accord with the latest fad. That tattoo was not very artistic or realistic either, an ugly bluish spot according to her. She had enquired her parents several times in disgust about that tattoo and got different conflicting stories at different times. Moreover, when she had interrogated about the truth behind it tallying those different responses from them, her parents had started quarrelling amongst themselves.

She stood up hurriedly, gripping the edge of the basin, spun the tap-head, took her cupped palms full of water and rubbed out the blood from the tattooed portion of her thigh. A pleasing smile lit up her face. However, her glowing white teeth looked diabolic on her blood covered face. She kneeled and kissed the tattoo as she finally knew its derivation; she loved it dearly now.

A few weeks ago

"Hello and welcome back; you are watching 'Morning News Hours'. I am Anirban Roy, bringing you the most talked about incidents in our state, West Bengal," the suited, gallant newsreader delivered his scripted dialogue as soon as the camera zoomed in on his face after the introductory music.

Ahi pushed away all the stuff she had dumped on the sofa, casually gluing her eyes on the television screen, and lounged in that tiny empty space she had just created. She picked up the remote control and increased the volume.

"No one would forget that evening of 15th April when that innocent girl was brutally raped and killed by four men. Our city, Kolkata has become the subject of utmost focus for not just the nation, but global attention after that shameful incident. Antara Chapi, a twenty-one-year-old girl from Mizoram came to Kolkata to accomplish her dream of being a singer. But who knew she would have to give up her life for her crime of dreaming. The name 'City of Joy' sounds like a slash on our pride, slap on our eminent culture and intellectuality. Five months have passed since that incident shook the nation and still those culprits are out there on the streets, roaming free. The opposition party is not missing any chance to gain a political advantage of this situation. And why not, when one of the accused rapists is the son of ruling party's MLA, Bakul Biswas. Candlelight vigils, obstinate positioning on the busy streets, setting government buses on fire, strikes, stopping trains and many others incidents are being reported from different parts of West Bengal as acts of protest. The normal people of the city have been deeply impacted by the vandalism of the opposition party cadres. However, today is the most awaited day of the verdict and the whole nation is waiting for the investigation report from Kolkata Police. Let me take you to the Lalbazar Police Station where our reporter, Timir Pal, is waiting to provide us the live updates," the newscaster accomplished his job of creating a grievous atmosphere.

The TV screen split into two parts to accommodate the reporter, breathlessly waiting for his turn to take centre stage.

"Timir, let our viewers know about the latest updates," the newsreader instructed.

"Anirban, as you can see behind me, media reporters from every nook and corner of the country are assembled here and waiting for Director General of Kolkata Police, Dhritiman Chatterjee to reveal the investigation report of that brutal incident. He can come out at any…." the correspondent continued in modulated voice with dramatic expression, trying his best to attract the viewers. However, not a single word pricked up Ahi's ears after the name, Dhritiman Chatterjee.

"Maa, come here! Hurry up! Baba on TV," Ahi shouted, excited.

All the reporters rushed to Dhritiman Chatterjee as soon as he stepped out of the police station. He was a six feet tall man in his late fifties, in a perfectly ironed uniform, heavily decorated with shining medals on his chest. Unlike his uniform, his clean-shaven, tanned and chiselled face had loose folds of skin between his jawline and throat, wrinkles around the eyes and grizzled hairs on the head. However, his wide shoulders and the well-built body was perfectly complimenting those medals. It was quite visible that he was still particular about his fitness regimen, even at this age.

Ahi flew a kiss, whispering, "My hero!"

"Kolkata Police has resolved the most-talked-about case of rape and murder of twenty-one-years-old Antra Chapi from Mizoram. We have successfully collected all the circumstantial and direct evidence which confirm the suspected four assailants are guilty, including Badal Biswas, the son of MLA Bakul Biswas. We have arrested all of them and interrogation will begin from today onwards," Dhritiman announced.

All the reporters started shooting their questions simultaneously.

"Please, one at a time. I can't hear any one of you," Dhritiman requested calmly. Few of his subordinate police officers took the onus to organize the conference. They instructed the reporters to raise their hand and ask their question only on Dhritiman's permission.

"Maa, are you coming or not?" Ahi screamed. Her mother pretended to be busy in her stint of the kitchen, ignoring Ahi.

"Sir, I would like to start my question referring William E. Gladstone's famous quote, 'Justice delayed is justice denied'. Don't you think this case is a perfect example of the quote?" One of the reporters asked to score some brownie points on behalf of her channel.

"I know this incident has deeply hurt our sentiment and social values. I have a daughter, almost the same age as Antara," Dhritiman responded followed by a momentary pause and continued, "I can understand the grief and trauma her parents are going through. But, emotion doesn't work in law and enforcement. We need evidence to give justice and it takes time, based on the complexity of circumstances."

"Sir, do you think Badal Biswas is one of the factors for this delay? As per the opposition leader's opinion, Kolkata Police is just a troop of slaves of the ruling party leaders and MLAs." Another reporter asked, attempting to prick a controversy.

Dhritiman smiled and replied, "I would like to refer to Socrates's famous quote here – 'Strong minds discuss ideas, average minds discuss events, weak minds discuss people'."

Ahi hopped on the sofa, whistling and ran to the kitchen.

"Maa, what's wrong?" Ahi enquired, embracing her from behind while she was busy in flipping the fish pieces on the fry-pan.

"Ahi! Can't you see this hot oil here?" she snapped back.

Ahi planted a kiss on her cheek and adorably babbled, "Ole baba le."

She was well conversant with her mother's concerns and tried her best on many past occasions to bring back her serenity. However, her mother just went back to her fancied vulnerability whenever Dhritiman took up any high-profile case. Moreover, it was not just a high-profile case then, as Dhritiman had arrested the only son of an influential politician of the city. Even after twenty-nine years of their marriage, she was not habituated of handling the pressure as the wife of a DGP.

"Maa, it's his job and we should be proud of him. He is serving our country, making our society safe," Ahi retorted firmly.

"And what about his family? Is it not his responsibility to keep his family safe first?" she screamed. Ahi attempted to respond, but her mother continued, not allowing her to utter a word, "Only his career, heroism, media appearances...these are important to him. He is completely indifferent to the fact that he is a father of a grown-up girl. Is it that he is the only person in town who should handle such cases and make enemies?"

Ahi gently pulled her to the sofa, and pushed her tenderly down onto it. Ahi kneeled down on the floor in front of her, sandwiched her mother's palm in between hers.

"Maa, I can understand your concern about my safety. But, the government does not work like that, right? Baba can't choose what case to work on and what not. His job is to keep this city safe and secure for its inhabitants and he is obliged to do whatever needs to be done to accomplish that." Ahi pleaded.

She pulled Ahi's face, cupping her face with her palms and kissed her on the forehead. After a moment of muteness, she started smirking, "Reality is much more unpredictable and wayward of law, order, right or wrong. You are young now; you will never really understand this until you have a daughter. Four years ago, Dhritiman had reopened a closed case and had arrested an industrialist. Few days after that, I had started getting abusive and threatening phone calls. One day, two men chased me home. Though Dhritiman took care of that chaos, but can you tell me why he had to reopen a closed case. Is there an answer for this?"

"He is just honest to his profession, Maa," Ahi replied.

"Leave it, neither you nor your baba will understand what I go through. Let me go, else my fish will burn. Get ready for office;

lunch is ready," she said, indifferent to Ahi's statement while she walked towards the kitchen.

"Maaa!" Ahi screamed, clenching her teeth as she could not find her cigarette packet in the glove compartment after her familiar groping, a couple of times from the driving seat.

She had been long addicted to nicotine since her college days. She had started smoking neither as a form of escapism from any estrangement, nor being compelled in college. Otaktay, the famous heinous, serial-killer protagonist from the bestseller novel, *Oozing Life* by Devang Awasthi inspired her to smoke. That novel engrossed her mind to such an extent that she had adopted a dangerous habit of inhaling a lung full of smoke and keeping herself submerged in the bathtub; just to assimilate the psychology of Otaktay and get beneath his skin. That was Otaktay's tactic to relish each moment of his life before committing any murder. It is needless to say that Ahi was an ardent admirer of author Devang Awasthi like millions of other Indians.

Ahi planned to stop by at a shop on the way to her office, outside the locality of her home to buy a cigarette packet. However, it started raining cats and dogs as soon her Beetle hit the road. Ahi couldn't take the risk of damaging her favourite twenty-fifth birthday gift from her parents as the wipers were miserably failing to give a clear vision. Only those Kolkata's yellow taxis were able to proclaim their existence through that curtain of water. She parked the car at the edge of a nearby pavement, pulled the handbrake and switched on the hazard lamp. Soon water stagnated on the surface of the street. Under the car hood it seemed like Ahi was sheltered in a bird watching hut, peeking out of the narrow window to watch the surface of the lake as the street became a riot of mini water plumes and concentric ripples.

That climate might have lit a pleasant smile on the farmers' faces, but definitely would be the reason of the frowns on the faces of Puja committees members as Durga puja was around the corner. All their efforts of the last few months were jeopardized. As per Hindu belief, every year Goddess Durga changes her mode of transportation. And heavy rains indicated that she was expected to arrive on a boat, which signifies good harvest, but at the same time, it means the possibility of a flood, which is not good for anybody.

"Fuck!" Ahi shrieked, banging on the steering wheel as she was late for office.

In spite of possessing a brilliant academic career which could have earned Ahi a high profile job, she had decided to open a publication house to converge her passion and profession. Dhritiman's reputation, associations in almost every lair of society and strong financial support made Ahi's journey to accomplish the dream, a sort of somnambulism. Samim and few of her other friends showed interest to be a part of her venture. She named the publication Ankur as they were still new as compared to eminent publications like Dolphin, Speaking Parrot and many others. However, Ahi had a positive perspective on that scenario as Ankur had an ample scope to grow and improve, as its very name suggested. They primarily started with debutant authors along with few already published articles, short stories and documents from famous authors as an accompaniment, so that Ankur could spread its roots deeper in the publishing industry, firming its existence. They had rented an office for Ankur at Park Street.

"Oops! The honourable founder is late today," Samim taunted as Ahi stepped inside the office.

Mohammad Samim Chaudhary was Ahi's childhood best friend. The journey of their friendship started while they were in the same class of kindergarten, and continued during their schooling and college. By profession, Samim was a radio jockey. His natural talent of voice modulation, sharp pronunciation, urban dialect, the unique texture of roughness in his voice, especially while expressing any emotion and producing witty, humour talks earned him many fans in the city. He had raised the bar high enough for the other RJs in the city. Lots of TV channels had also offered him the role of anchoring in different reality shows and news. However, he was not interested. He had a strange conviction that a radio-man should always be invisible to the listeners as it offers plenty of scope for the listeners to fantasize about the man behind the voice. According to Ahi, Samim's persuasion was just an excuse to hide his incapability to charm people by his appearance, as he was a man of average built and height with round face in a crew-cut hair style and had an innocent, dreamy pair of eyes which was completely out of sync with his masculine voice.

Ahi kept her bag on her desk, picked up her water bottle and walked away towards the pantry. Samim followed her.

Samim snatched the water bottle from Ahi, held it like a loudspeaker and started dramatically, "People of Kolkata can expect a clear sky very soon. But somewhere, in someone's heart still, it is thundering. Yes, we can..."

Ahi muted him placing her palm on his face and said irritatingly, "Enough!" She grasped the bottle hastily from his hand and placed it under the filter.

"May I know the weather report please?" Samim asked sarcastically.

"Samim, please keep all these kind of jokes for your listeners, housewives with the mid-life crisis," Ahi retorted, tightening the cap of the bottle.

It was an unsaid game called 'tease-me-if-you-can'. And Samim was the undefeated winner so far as he knew Ahi more than anyone else.

"Jah! I have fans from all the age groups. Kolkata doesn't leave the bed before listening to Samim, the man with the magical voice," Samim replied like an unbeaten champion of that game, tugging his collar upwards.

"Huh! *Ladkhor Bangali sob* (all lazy Bengalis), they just need an excuse to pass time uselessly," Ahi said, returning to her desk. He followed her.

Ahi arranged her laptop, reaching her desk and settled on her chair to start work.

"Ahem!" Samim cleared his throat.

Ahi was well acquainted what Samim was about to say after that. Hence, she warned him in advance, pointing her index finger at him, "Please! I am in a very bad mood, Samim."

"Okay fine! But I am not missing the sun at all," Samim stated.

"Why?" Ahi asked as a formality, inattentively, checking her emails.

"You are looking hot like a sunny, warm and sweaty day in this skin-tight, orange top," Samim leaped across her cubical immediately. She showed her middle finger followed by a silent lip gesture to convey 'Fuck you'. Samim left for his desk, giggling.

Ahi had grown up showered with affection and attention from her parents and relatives. She always enjoyed listening to praises about her beauty from people in childhood. However, her charismatic appearance became her primary obstacle to spread her wings. Her so-called well-wishers started advising her parents to keep her under observation. And as a result, she completely lost her freedom. She had a sculpted figure. Her pair of thin, coal-black and arched eyebrows eased down gently to her black, feathery long eyelashes. The sea-greenish eyeballs of her widely-extended pair of eyes perfectly complimented her milky-white complexion. The boy-cut hair, haphazardly leaving long locks over her pink cheeks, partly coved her delicate, small ears. Her smile revealing those glittering white teeth in between rosy, heart-shaped lips could beguile any man.

Eventually, she noticed a white envelope on her desk as she looked up from her laptop screen. She could not believe her eyes, reading the sender's name written on that envelope. She was thrilled enough to get a run of goose bumps all over her body. Her pink skin turned red near her nose and tender ears. Her hand quivered, picking up the envelope from the desk.

Ahi was a bibliophile from childhood. Whatever might be the occasion – her birthday, Durga Puja, her parents' anniversary or their birthdays – she always had managed to get books from her relatives and family.

The young Belgian reporter and adventurer, Tintin; the magical world of the young wizard, Harry Potter and his friends; extremely intelligent Chacha Chowdhary; romping and mischievous students Nonte and Fonte and many others like them had made little Ahi's puerility a cheerful journey. Her parents had never tried to be intruders in her world of books as the textbooks of her syllabi were equally her favourite. Gradually, those children's books took the backseat of her bookshelves, leaving their territory for Rabindranath Tagore, Stephen King, Sharadindu Bandyopadhyay, Paulo Coelho, Sarat Chandra Chattopadhyay and many more eternally famed novelists and poets. The overnight sensation Devang Awasthi earned a special place in her collection because of his philosophically rich, grey-shaded characters with human flaws, which always attracted her.

She loved to read different types of books, irrespective of the subject or genre. She was addicted to tactual sensation, derived from the texture of book's pages and its smell always satiated her olfactory organ. Her addiction eventually transformed her room into a Bibliotheca; books, coffee, and cigarettes were the three indispensables for her.

"Don't tell me this is your prank!" Ahi warned, glowering and shaking the envelope close to Samim's face. Everyone in the office were aware of his pranks and mischievous character.

Samim pulled Ahi, grabbing her hand, guided her to sit on the chair in front of him and crooned, "Shhhh! Calm down. I did not do anything."

"Then why were you fucking grinning?" she asked clenching her jaw in a low voice.

"These are my face-muscles baby; out of my control. They just start working out whenever I see my sunshine in front of me," Samim flirted.

"Can't you be serious for a second?" she asked failing miserably to conceal her smile.

Samim snatched the envelope from her hand and read the sender's name, written on the envelope. Flipping both sides of the envelope a couple of times, he said, "This is not possible." Ahi opened her mouth in an attempt to protest, but Samim continued, "Ahi, just think logically. Why will a celebrity author like Devang Awasthi approach Ankur? So far, all his five novels have sold in millions. Three of them are already picked up for Bollywood mainstream movies. Give me one reason."

Ahi pouted, followed by a pseudo whimper, "I know, I am a devotee of his writings. He is a doctor by profession."

"Then you should know that he expired two months back," Samim informed.

"Oh yes! I remember now. He had committed suicide a few months back. It just went out of mind in excitement," Ahi told in a low voice, almost under her breath.

"Do you remember any other news except uncle's press conference?" Samim teased.

"Oh god! I can't think anymore. Let's go for a smoke. I am dying for nicotine since morning."

They went out of the office premises and approached their smoking area by the street.

"Isn't it possible that one of his relatives, friend or family might have sent that manuscript?" Ahi asked on the way. Samim frowned looking at her. "Ju… Just hypothetically, isn't it logical?" Ahi fumbled. Samim kept walking, ignoring her prate.

The arrogant and restless clouds seemed to have vowed to drown the city that day. Ahi looked outside through her bedroom's window to find the glittering raindrops under the tall lampposts taking the shape of a shower. Vehicles were passing cautiously, with their hazard-lamps on. She relished the view briefly with tiny sips of hot coffee before getting to that suspicious manuscript.

She changed her mind and decided to head home and read it in the tranquility of her room.

Returning home, she was enjoying the long discussion with her father regarding the success of his recent investigation. However, she was desperate to riffle through those papers. She pulled out the envelope, a cigarette packet and a lighter from her bagpack and placed them on her study table by her favourite blue coffee mug which had 'Kindly go away, I'm Reading' written on it. She tore the envelope carefully. Her hand shook as she was startled by a sudden sound of thunder. "Fuck!" she exclaimed, gritting her teeth.

She lit a cigarette and started reading.

According to famous American author Napoleon Hill, any human behaviour can be explained by eight basic motives – Love, materialism, sex, self-preservation, freedom of body and mind, revenge, self-expression and life after death. However, this explanation was never enough to preserve social harmony and safety. Hence, we constructed constitutions, laws and enforcements to establish impartiality across the barriers of religions, castes, financial diversities or physical strengths. We introduced several social convictions as well like marriage and family to distribute the pleasure and affection, irrespective of deservedness; to restrict the alpha males or females. The intent of all these rules and restrictions were to fail the Darwinian evolutionary theory of natural selection, 'Survival of the fittest'.

Did we get success in our intention? No, we are still following Darwin's theory. Moreover, we are adulterating the limpidness of natural selection. According to the theory, the individual best adapted to the circumstances and achiever of reproductive success will preserve the favoured race in the struggle for life and that was a necessity.

But we redefined the meaning of 'fittest' as authoritative – politically, financially, influentially or religiously. And these fittest people use their dominance for greed which can never be justified as a necessity.

Nature was biased while creating fauna; gifted humans a much more improved and complicated organ called the brain. The brain had equipped humans to inhibit over the rest of the fauna and make them slaves. Though they were much fitter to adapt to nature and much stronger to mash the human race, they were defeated by the human brain. However, this sovereignty could not satisfy the craftiest creation of nature, and they started shedding blood among themselves, forming different groups. Nature gifted all of us one sun, one moon, same water, land, and sky, but we covered our eyes in different colours of political, religious, regional and linguistic franchise to discriminate them and their interpretations. Eventually, that separation narrowed down to individual human beings, and in the current scenario, any two humans can be separated based on several scales like nationality, religion, caste, language, colour, financial background, political perception and many other innumerable conspiracies of the human brain.

I was one of those 'fittest' who could go to any extent for self-interest and realistic rationalization.

According to my relatives, friends and acquaintances, I was lucky to get the title 'Awasthi' after my name. They were not wrong completely; even I might have thought the same if I would have been in their place. They just saw the finest clothes I wore that money could buy in India, the Audi Q7 to drop me to school and college, my expensive accessories and gadgets. I was the sole inheritor of the enormous property of Devaraj Awasthi, including Awasthi Medical College and Hospital and three other luxurious hospitals. However, they missed noticing the blood accidentally oozing out from the hidden wound under those expensive clothes, my moist eyes behind those dark-tinted glasses of the car, my aloofness to those luxurious accessories and gadgets and my unfathomable depression.

I had lost my mother a few hours after my birth and was brought up with the stigma of being my own mother's killer. My name was a by-word of scorn and opprobrium to all my relatives. Hence, I was left alone even in family gatherings or functions. My father, Devraj Awasthi had exploited that opportunity to craft his ultimate business-machine to win the monopolisation of medical-business, turning me into an emotionless robot. My father, no, 'My master' would be the proper words to address him, never allowed me to do even any insignificant mistake in studies or in obeying his rules. I was never allowed to be second in my class. If in case I failed to stand first, my ripped flesh always reminded me of the difference between my marks and the highest marks, obtained by the other student.

That day is still vivid in my memory. Master called me to his study room, the first room on the left after crossing the giant drawing room on the ground floor. Big industrialists, famous doctors and influential political personalities used to gather in that room on every alternate weekend. They used to discuss business, rather I'd say conspire to loot innocent, common citizens till late nights.

My teenaged, scrawny legs shivered while stepping inside that room.

"Come to me!" he called politely, lighting his face with a pleasant smile and spreading his arms. Momentarily, I felt pampered and secure to see him smiling. I ran towards him to surrender myself in his arms. My mother seemed happy as I peeped at her colossal portrait on the wall over Master's shoulder. I had seen her only in that portrait.

"You did a good job," he whispered in my ear, patting my back. He freed me from his arms to see my face, "But you should have done better."

"Have you heard the name, Buzz Aldrin?" He asked while he started unbuttoning my shirt. I shook my head, looking puzzled.

"Not your fault at all. Many of us don't know him. Unfortunately, he was the second human to step on the moon; Neil Alden Armstrong was the first human and we all remember his name," he continued, taking off my shirt.

He grabbed my hand and took me to the white wall, exactly opposite of the wall where my mother's portrait was fastened.

"Stand here, facing the wall," he ordered pointing towards the wall. All my sense organs, except eyes, were trying hard to conjecture his activity behind me. "Today, I will start your training to be a superior human being," he continued. I could sense that he was going away from me as his voice was becoming softer gradually and then the clang of metal pricked my ears, making it tough for my eyes to stick to that white wall. "You will thank me when you will be mature enough to understand me," he said. I could hear his voice closer to my ears.

Something coarse and thin bit my right shoulder and the rest of its tail slapped my chest. I looked down on my chest, but before my speculative brain could identify that object, it disappeared, scratching my skin deeply. My central nervous system – which is made up of the spinal cord and brain was – unrehearsed to accept any such message of that ruthless strike from my peripheral nervous system. I lost my senses and fell down on the floor. He continued his drill of 'making-superior-human' every time, whenever I failed to meet his expectations. Every time, I stood in front of that white wall, naked, and tolerated Master's malicious wish, I studied each and every minute detail of that white wall. It was a mere white wall for everyone; only I could see a lot of faces, colours, nature and a whole world on it. I could see my mother there, cuddling my face, kissing me all over. That must have been an illusion created by my brain to escape from that unendurable pain of whipping.

Ahi flipped the page with moist eyes. She squeezed the cigarette butt against the ashtray in habituated fumbling, gluing her eyes on the manuscript and started reading,

My puerility had spent in desperate efforts to escape from Master's whips. Everyone is scared of darkness, but it was my cocoon of comfort as I could hide my scars of shame which used to proclaim my defeat. Darkness had helped me to avert the human in the mirror I hated the most. I started hating everything around me, even my existence.

Sometimes, blood used to ooze from my wounds, leaving stains on my bed sheets and clothes. As I was a novice to bandage my own wound without the mirror, in course of circumstances, one of our maids, Mira aunty, noticed those stains while washing them. Out of curiosity, she peeped at me while I was changing to find my bloody wounds and enquired about them. I kept my mouth shut as that was the only way to avoid Master's anger. She prodded and eventually I spilled out all to her, being lured by her motherly affection. My innocent mind and benevolent heart were poor at the game of camouflage.

She started pampering me like a mother does to his son, helping me to bandage and dress my wounds, feed me, iron my school uniform and so on. She perfectly filled the absence of my mother and my dependency on her gradually increased. The love, affection, and bonding of a mother with her child are the strongest in nature among all kinds of relationship of our society. The love and bonding I used to share with Mira aunty was spurred by the simplest emotion of being human.

Human emotions are not based on concepts, whether it is love, hate or any other derived one from these two primary emotions. They are the controllers of our actions in real, so was Mira aunty's. Master's brutality had been conglomerating a grudge in her mind. One day, that which I was always afraid of took place. I was afraid of losing her forever. She invaded into Master's study room without his permission, tugging me along with her and shouted at the top of her voice. Master didn't answer any of her questions; neither did he try to justify his actions. He just smiled.

I did not see Mira aunty again in my life after that day, and was punished cruelly.

Human interaction is the basic and natural demeanour of human attributes and that was the hardest pretension for me. I was a loner even in a crowd. After Mira aunty departed from my life, I was always scared of sharing the smallest part of my life with others. I could not make any friends, neither in school, nor in college. Gradually, numbness became a static state of my mind when I had completed my medical study. Those humans who came close to me circumstantially, like Mira aunty, had to part due to some other series of circumstances that were out of my control. I was like those floating objects which effortlessly reach the seashore surfing on the crest of the waves and are yanked along with the same waves to the deep of the sea. The wave never asks those object's wish.

The rain had stopped outside and there was pin drop silence inside the room except for the plopping sound of water drops falling into the stagnant water in the balcony's tree-tub. A cool breeze brushed Ahi's bare neck. She turned back hastily to find the window open. A couple of sudden knocks on the door startled Ahi.

"Who is that?" she asked, almost screaming in shock.

"Ahi, it is one-thirty in the night! Why are you still awake?" Relief brought a smile on Ahi's face, as she heard her mother's voice from outside. Ahi was a little scared, though she was unclear why, as she was a brave girl. Moreover, on many occasions when she went to watch horror movies with Samim, she found those movies funny rather than scary.

"Maa, I had some work to finish. You just go to sleep; I will sleep in a few minutes."

"Okay, but I will come back again to check," she warned.

Ahi sighed, switched off the light and hit the hay. She kept her eyes closed, trying hard to drift off to sleep, but could not. She opened her eyes to find the manuscript, vivid under the faint but beaming light, coming through the window from outside. She got up abruptly in discomfort. She walked down to her bookshelves and took out one of Devang Awasthi's books. She had seen his deep pair of eyes beneath that black, square-framed spectacles, neatly back-combed pitch-black hair and stubbly face complimenting his wide and firm jaws several times before. But, that night Ahi found that picture on the back cover much different than before – more intense, alive, expressing and breathing like an impression in a mirror.

A strange, eerie feeling kept her awake throughout the night.

Next morning, as soon as Samim reached his desk, Ahi slammed the manuscript on his desk and whispered leaning close to his face, "We have to publish this!"

"Not again, please," Samim sighed, smirking.

"Samim, you will not believe what the fuck is there in this manuscript," Ahi said with immense enthusiasm, shaking him by his shoulder.

"Have you ever heard about Devang Awasthi's personal life anywhere?" she asked, beaming her glowing eyes in ebullience.

"Personal life? He did not open his mouth even when he was accused of human organ trafficking; he was always reluctant to come in front of the media and I had heard he was addicted to some drug as well. Even after his death, there was not much news," he said.

"Exactly! Here, he has described his personal life in detail, candidly. Can you imagine the demand, if this gets published in the market?" Ahi exclaimed, hopping on her toes.

"And who will believe that? Come out of your dream, Ahi. A guy who did not speak in the deep crisis of his life had written his life story and sent to you for publishing before his death? Bullshit," he retorted offloading his shoulder, keeping his bag on the desk. "We cannot publish this manuscript until he signs our agreement and that is not possible. I am warning you Ahi, we can fall into a big legal soup," he added.

A gloomy depression overcast Ahi's lit-up face. She bent her head towards the floor and whispered, "But, I know his style of writing. No one can craft this masterpiece; it is definitely him."

"Uff!" he exhaled heavily.

"I know; it is not making any sense. But..." she pouted at the end of her cadence where her voice fell into a mute.

After a few silent moments, Samim said, wrapping his voice in a pseudo angry expression, "Come on, I thought I'd get a gift today and you are obsessed with that anonymous manuscript. Nobody cares about me; not even you."

Samim just hated to see Ahi depressed.

"Today is not your birthday," she recalled thoughtfully, frowned.

"How can you forget? Today is our anniversary; you did kiss me on this very same day for the first time," Samim whined with a dramatic expression.

"Oh god! That happened ten years back, for the first and the last time. I was a kiddo then. I just wanted to experience that feeling after reading a novel; that is it," she retorted.

"But you did say, I love you," he argued to prove his point.

"Because it was written in that novel," Ahi answered with a failed attempt to control her laugh. Samim laughed, clapping.

It was a busy day for all of them in office as Ankur Publications had decided to launch a new magazine to celebrate Durga Puja. The challenge was quite tough for them as there were few popular and well-established magazines in the market. Bengalis could not even think of Durga Puja without those magazines. Hence, Ahi and her team had decided to work hard to achieve the ultimate perfection for the puja edition, concentrating on the selection of stories, articles and poems, editing, cover designing and convincing sponsors for puja related advertisements.

"Ahi, Pranab sir was looking for you," Rupali, an enthusiastic, young intern informed, panting.

"What the hell? Is everything okay? Why are you huffing like this?" Ahi enquired.

"Pranab sir asked me to call you immediately. I came to your desk a few minutes back, but you were not here," Rupali said, gradually taking control over her rapid breathing.

Ahi smiled, "Okay, I will meet him." Rupali left, happy to have accomplished her task.

Pranab Bose was the co-founder of Ankur Publications and the former chief editor of the leading national newspaper, *The Indian Era*. He had experience of almost twenty years in the publication and mass communication industry. It was his name that earned Ankur Publications weightage in Indian literature. However, his fame and experience made him arrogant, sharpening his dictatorial characteristics.

Though Ahi was not his devotee like her other colleagues, she always respected Pranab for his precious experience, knowledge, and repute.

"Sir, may I come in?" Ahi asked, partly opening the door of his cabin.

"Yes, please," Pranab responded, his eyes glued on a newspaper. His typical nerdish appearance in a Johor-coat over a long kurta, thick and black-framed spectacles, salt and pepper beard and hair could convince any rookie writer of self-rejection.

"Do we have any legitimacy of this piece of work?" he asked immediately after Ahi sat on a chair opposite to him.

Ahi expected him to ask such questions when she had sent the email to Pranab seeking his permission to publish the manuscript. Hence, she had prepared a convincing answer.

"That won't be a problem. We can get a signature from any of his family members in his absence."

"Have you tried to contact any of them?" he asked indifferently, flipping the page of that newspaper.

"Yes, I called his home number and talked to his wife. She is not interested in publishing or discussing anything about his writing. But, I believe, I can convince her," Ahi replied, fumbling.

Pranab folded the newspaper delicately, tossed it on the table, and looked at her face. "Ahi, it's not a joke. As you mentioned in your email, this manuscript is kind of an autobiography; an autobiography of a celebrity."

Ahi nodded like an obedient student.

"We can't publish this; it's a 'no' from my side. Do you have any idea about section 499 and 500 of the Indian Penal Code?" he asked, leaning his face close to Ahi.

"No," Ahi responded in shock.

"Oh no! Who am I asking? You are the daughter of Mr Dhritiman Chatterjee, but you know what, I don't have such strong influence. Hence, law and order is not so negligible for me," he said lounging comfortably on his push-back chair.

Ahi's earlobe and nostril turned red. She was intolerant being identified by her father's position.

"And what if I can manage a written permission from his family?" she asked almost whispering as the anger and humiliation boiled up inside her.

"A written permission from a core member of his family, not any random relative," he replied, turning his face to the laptop. He added, "I must advise you to concentrate on the puja edition rather than chasing an anonymous manuscript."

She stomped out of the cabin. She vowed to publish that manuscript at any cost, gradually toughening her heart with each step towards her desk. She took a deep breath, and after reaching her desk, murmured, "I have my own identity."

Ahi reached home late at night; even her father had returned before Ahi that day. She stepped out of her car to open the iron gate in front of her house. She did not honk that day to call the security person as she did not want to disturb her neighbours.

Ahi stopped suddenly while approaching the gate, startled by an unusual vision behind her. She turned back to find a human silhouette just in front of the nearest lamp post. It seemed like a waste basket and a garbage bag resting on top of it. She smiled in relief, exhaling. She walked back towards the gate, swung open the latch and pushed the gate gently. She wondered about the height of that garbage can. "Isn't it a bit too tall?" she mumbled to herself. Instead of driving the car into the parking, she walked towards the dustbin again hurriedly. She stopped with a stumble as that waste basket moved backward. She felt a heavy thump of her heart and a chill blew through her spine. The waste basket turned into a prominent human silhouette then with a clearly distinguishable torso, limbs, and head. A woman, as Ahi guessed from the structural attributes. After a few unnerving moments, that woman departed and vanished in the darkness. Ahi kept standing there, perplexedly until her mother called from the second floor's window.

That night she skipped dinner, making an excuse of a stomach upset and locked herself in her room as early as possible to start reading the manuscript. She gathered all her stuff to ignite her reader's mode and started reading.

I had just returned from the United Kingdom, finishing my specialization in gynaecology and had taken over the responsibility of Master's hospitals. The foreign degrees after my name had sharpened Master's weapon to wrangle difficult business deals from his competitors. Though during my study in the United Kingdom, I was out of Master's control, I could not completely purify my blood from his slavery.

That night, I was busy in preparing a presentation for the new investors. I was quite tensed and under pressure to meet the granted time deadline, maintaining quality as per Master's satisfaction. But

I was finding it difficult to concentrate on my work as I could hear people quarrelling outside my cabin. I came out of my cabin, annoyed to find a clique, desperate to win some war of word over each other. I trotted to them aggressively.

Two doctors and a security guard who were the part of the tiny crowd became silent after realizing my presence. And the rest were unknown people, huddling around a badly injured boy on a stretcher, and were not speaking either. The only arrogant warrior of that word-war was a nurse who was not ready to give up.

"Can't you see how this little boy is suffering?" she hollered in concern. The boy was bleeding severely, making a puddle of blood on the stretcher.

"Sir, we can't treat him without reporting to the police as it's a road accident," one of the doctors informed, reading the speculation on my face while I looked at him. "And none of these people know this boy personally," another doctor added.

FIR or first information report of police was never mandatory to start treatment or admit an injured person in the hospital. Moreover, as per Indian laws, it is the liability of any government or private medical institution to furnish initial treatment to an injured in a road accident and not to harass the good Samaritans who bring them to the hospital. However, having consistent laws and rules in place is one thing, having them properly implemented is another, as the implementation part is always controlled by the fittest people of our society for their personal interest. The actual intention of having a copy of the FIR before taking any kind of action is a mechanism to identify the potential customer who will be bearing the cost of the medical treatment.

"I will bear the cost if no one comes forward later. You can deduct the amount from my salary, sir," the nurse proposed.

Her stretched and eloquent pair of eyes were courageous, confident in gumption, bright in truth and moist in compassion. She was a real warrior not only in words, as I knew the scrawny salary of a nurse was insufficient to cover the colossal medical bills. She was driven by intuition as she completely snubbed the reality of her inability to pay that bill. Her name badge read: Sanjivani Shukla. What a perfect name she had, Sanjivani, that magical plant which can awake the dead people to life and lend immortality. She had tanned skin and it was obvious from her appearance that she was least bothered about her appearance and must have spent a long period of her life in the struggle for existence. Her wide jawline was proclaiming the sense of responsibility. The nursing cap on her head seemed like a crown of a warrior queen.

I was attracted to those aspects of her character. I requested Sanjivani to bring that boy into the operation theatre and ordered the doctors to start their treatment. They obeyed me reluctantly.

No, I was never a hero; neither was I trying to be one. She must have had a moral intention behind her stand. However, for me, it was just an act of sabotage against my father. It was her eyes spurred me that night to disregard the hospital's rule; more specifically my father's rule. Yes, the first time in my life, I failed Awasthi Medical College and Hospital (AMCH) that night in my complete cognizance. She had that magical power to make me brave enough to stand against my father and complete my masculinity. I felt an immense craving to bring her into my life.

Ahi turned the page with a pleasant smile, sensing some divine romance in the next pages.

Of course, my father whipped me brutally for that incident, but it was satiating for me. I could feel his pain of being defeated by one of his weakest slaves, while he was trying hard to exceed his physical ability to rip my flesh. The memory of Sanjivani's restless eyeballs, quivering eyelashes, nervous lips biting, squeaky and thin neck and oscillating earrings nurtured an immunity in my core to tolerate those brutal lashes.

My father fired Sanjivani, the only earning member of her poor family. It was impossible for anyone to get a job in other hospitals, being sacked from AMCH. I started helping her financially by taking care of her parents. She refused initially due to her self-esteem. However, circumstances were such that she had to accept my help. They were in wretched financial condition; but they were rich in affection, in respecting relations and in prioritizing human emotions and liberties over materialism. Her parents were insalubrious; but healthy enough to raise their child with enough love. She was blessed to have a perfect family; not cursed like me.

We started counting on each other in different aspects.

My bringing up had taught me only two emotions, fear and embarrassment. For the first time in my life, I had felt the presence of other emotions in the core of my senses and basked in the affectionate touch of a woman when she stepped into my life. She had opened the door to a new world which I had been otherwise deprived of. However, she was not the first woman to touch me sexually. I had lost my virginity during puberty, when Master caught me masturbating and took me to a brothel. I had no freedom to relish my personal visualization of pleasure. According to him, it was just a biological necessity and a successful man should not have any weakness on that unproductive activity. Moreover, a doctor should consider a human body as subject, irrespective of gender. He killed all my curiosity and fantasy about sex before my pubescence.

Sex is never only a physical pleasure to me as all our physical activities are controlled by the brain; mental pleasance plays the main role in this act. Those mental delights come through watching the bliss in your partner's eyes, savouring the sensation of inadvertent touches on the skin, intense pressure on muscles, gentle bites and haphazard fellate, through feeling the indulgence your partner feels, and through basking equal possession of each other's body and soul. I never felt any resonance with those elderly women of the brothel. Their predictable, callous and tedious movements always failed to draw my brain in the play and I too had started believing Master's perspective. Eventually, I had stopped visiting them and started pursuing a celibate life for almost fifteen years, till I had met Sanjivani. She redefined that 'unproductive biological necessity' as a gratifying treat to my soul, body, senses, and existence.

We wished to have each other in our lives. Though for me the legal approval was enough for our relation, she always desired to have a consent of society, and so of our religious franchise. My Master's disapprobation on my marriage was quite obvious. How could he just unprofitably give away his most expensive product? There was a huge business plan beneath his investment in making me emotionally numb, a cold-blooded human, addicted to prostitutes and the most successful doctor in the city. So, I could marry the mentally challenged daughter of the richest industrialist of that time and draw innumerable investments for his expanding empire. As that industrialist was ready to bear the expenditures for Master's future projects, just to hide his social stigma.

I was addicted to that lavish luxurious lifestyle. I couldn't fly away with Sanjivani to struggle for our existence. That perilous circumstance resulted in a fatal plan in my mind. All our actions are born in our mind first and our life is just the physical manifestation of our thoughts. Eventually, I had attracted that situation in reality to execute my long-craved plan.

That night, Master called me in his room when he learnt about my court marriage with Sanjivani. That was my punishment room, the first one on the left after crossing the drawing room on the ground floor.

He swallowed a peg of whiskey in on breath and ordered calmly, "Take off your all clothes and stand, facing the wall."

I stood in front of that white wall, expecting to meet those humans who always provided me the strength. To my surprise, a hot metal touched my buttocks, and within a fraction of a second that metal struck, to rip my bum's flesh apart. I screamed, spitting out. That was not a whip, I realized. He chose the same place again for the second strike. I lost my senses slightly and could see those necked humans vividly on that white wall in front me. They were crying in commiseration. I saw my wounds and the blood on them.

"How dare you ruin my business!" he shouted on top his voice and blew that metal on the same spot.

Blood reached to the carpet, trickling down my thighs and legs. I saw Sanjivani in that crowd on the wall. She came close to me, flying on her two long feathery wings and kissed my lips.

"I will make you impotent today, so your emotion can't erupt anymore stup…." His voice slurred all of a sudden. The little girl who was crying inconsolably on the wall till then, started laughing vigorously, pointing towards Master. I turned around to find him

collapsed on the floor. Might be a plaque, an accumulation of cholesterol, white blood cells and calcium had broken inside his coronary artery and formed a blood clot. He stretched his hand for help and gestured to me to bring his medicines from the cupboard. I stood there like a statue to visualize the narrowing of his artery, which blocked the oxygen flow in his heart. He crawled for a couple of minutes to reach the cupboard. I took all his medicines and walked away to the farthest corner of the room. His eyes bulged out of his contorted face. Few more seconds to go, till his heart could pump the blood using the left-out oxygen in his artery. He was the great teacher to teach me that complex organ of human body – heart. Gradually, his feeble body abnegated to obey his wish, accepting the defeat from karma and invited my freedom of life. Sometimes, being brutal to others becomes an act of mercy on oneself; unfortunately, the other person was my father. He died. Rather, I should say, I had committed patricide.

Ahi had a glance at the clock before turning the page; it showed half past one in the morning. She wiped her moist eyes, sighing. Her sleep-deprived eyes were not ready to function anymore. But she could not help but read till the end.

Fire is one of the holiest and purest forms of nature, along with wind, soil and water. I am an atheist, but if I must admire something as god, these four would be my mysticisms. However, the biggest atheists are those who do business with the beliefs of theists under various religious franchises in temples, mosques, churches, gurudwaras and other religious stores. My father's corpse was placed on the perfectly arranged pyre, waiting for the divine touch of fire. I wore a depressed mask on my face to hide my jovial heart and my shades came handy to conceal my eloquent eyes. I believe, there were many people like me in that gathered crowd who made an effort to disguise their true feelings. However, they all were in white uniform. There are many differences between our image in other's eyes and our image in the mirror. Those differences are collectively called camouflage, the trickiest creations of nature, the biggest blessing and curse for human beings. Gradually, I became an exponent of that art. Hence, Sanjivani never could know the secret of her happiness. Yes, our happy married life was built on a lie. The lie, truth, good and bad all are just relative perceptions of our camouflaged mind.

After the purohit had finished his mantras and rituals, I lit the fire on that pyre. The fire spread over that wooden heap. The light wind and ghee had catalysed the procedure of cremation. Fire burns everything into ashes, unbiased by race or religion, unlike other human manifested gods. I kept my father's ashes with me instead of pouring it in the river as the part of rituals. It helps me to face the obstacles of my life, reminding me of the darkest period of my life.

Ahi closed her eyes, forcing her tears to roll down her face. She left her chair and approached her parents' room stealthily. They were in deep sleep. Ahi walked close to their bed and leaned close to their face as they were not prominently visible in that dim and green night lamp. They were looking like kids – innocent, calm and relaxed, relishing the warmth, comfort and softness of the bed. Ahi delicately touched her lips on her mother's forehead.

"Umm!" her mother mumbled, frowned.

She kissed her father before leaving the room, thanking god for gifting her a perfect life.

A hi woke up with a headache; her tired eyes were burning and watering. She felt pain in all her joints. She was burning up in fever. She wrapped herself tightly in the bed sheet. She was trying hard to behave normally as she did not want her mother to know about her sickness.

She picked up her mobile, only stretching her hand out of the bed sheet after a couple of rings. She responded in low voice, "Hello?"

"Are not you coming today? It's 1:30 p.m," Samim's voice asked.

"Yes, I will come, but a little late, I am feverish," she replied in a hushed voice so that her mother could not hear.

"You are not going anywhere today; get up and have this tablet," Ahi's mother ordered as she entered the room. "When I came to wake you up in the morning, I noticed your fever. I switched off the fan. I was just waiting for you to wake up," she added.

"Samim, I will call you back in a few minutes," Ahi informed and hung up.

"Don't listen to me, I am your enemy, right? I warned you not to stay awake till late in the night. But no, you have to finish all your work in one night. You are not getting out of your bed," Ahi's mother continued.

Ahi swallowed the pill and her mother's grumbling with water, making a puppy face. Ahi had to calm her anger. Ahi called Samim as soon as her mother left the room.

"Samim, book an evening flight ticket for me to Delhi and mail the itinerary," Ahi almost whispered in one breath.

"Aren't you sick? And why Delhi? What is wrong with you?" Samim quizzed.

"Samim, we have to publish this manuscript. If not the author's signature, then I will get the signature of someone from his family," Ahi answered.

"That's fine, but you are unwell. On top of that, we have so much stuff to wrap up before Durga Puja. We have only one-and-a-half weeks in hand. We can do this even after Durga Puja; what is the hurry?" Samim tried to read her mind.

"Not sure, but I am scared that I'll lose that manuscript; it has the potential to give our publication a huge take-off. And I know you guys can efficiently manage the Puja edition," Ahi replied slowly and thoughtfully.

"But…" Samim attempted to object but Ahi emphasised, not allowing him to talk, "No ifs and buts! Okay bye, Maa is coming back."

Ahi's mother entered the room, carrying a plate and ordered, "Go and brush your teeth."

"Maa, I won't eat this boiled potato and rice. It's full of carbohydrates," Ahi nagged, making a face.

"*Kono nekami noi* (no drama). I just had a discussion with Jayanta and he suggested this. I should see an empty plate when I get back," her mother admonished.

A pleasant smile lit Ahi's face as she heard the name of their family physician and her father's friend, Jayanta. He was Ahi's only hope. She called him.

"Hello Jayanta uncle, please make Maa understand that I am perfectly okay. I have to fly to Delhi tonight for my work and only you can get me the permission. Please! please! please!" Ahi pleaded in one breath.

"Okay, I will. I will stop by your home on the way to my clinic," he assured, laughing.

Samim parked his bike in a hurry and ran towards the departure gates. Netaji Subhas Chandra Bose International Airport was the fifth busiest airport in India, where more than ten million passengers travel through each year. Moreover, the auspicious occasion of Durga Puja had transformed the airport into a sea of people. Middle-class Bengalis save up throughout the year so that they can go on holidays during Durga Puja, while those Bengalis who stay away from their homes for work or study, come back to celebrate this festival with their families. Samim had to comb the entire airport to find Ahi and her parents.

"Uff finally!" Ahi sighed, seeing Samim approaching them.

"Ahi, you won't believe the traffic jam and water logging, especially that junction of VIP road. I started almost two hours back from office," Samim explained.

"Tell me about it," Ahi's father, Dhritiman expressed his disgust. "Anyway, Ahi, the queue is too long; go and get your boarding pass," he added.

"Wait, have you taken your medicines?" Ahi's mother enquired. Ahi nodded.

"Oh-ho, she will miss the flight now; let her go," Dhritiman objected. Ahi's mother hushed, glowering at her husband as Ahi touched her parents' feet, hugged Samim and went inside the airport.

"You will be responsible if she falls sick again," Ahi's mother admonished, pointing her index finger at Dhritiman. The Director General of Kolkata Police, the fright for the criminals and lawbreakers of Kolkata, fumbled, consoling his angry wife, "She... she can buy the medicines after reaching there as well. Right?"

Ahi waved to them after collecting her boarding pass; they waved back till she vanished in the queue for security check.

"Wait here, I will get the car," Dhritiman instructed and walked towards the parking lot. Samim now had Ahi's mother as company, but he soon realised that it was a bad decision to wait with her when she asked, "What's your future plan?"

He answered, fumbling, "Got a few opportunities in television... anchoring, aunty. So, working... working hard to groom myself a bit before shooting starts."

"Good! And what about marriage?" she darted.

"Marriage? Have not thought about that yet." Samim was clueless.

"What do you mean? What are you guys waiting for? You know each other since childhood, right?" she asked, concerned. "But what is this nonsense, travelling so far in weak health? I just can't take this anymore," she continued. Samim nodded, desperately waiting for Dhritiman to return.

"Samim, I want a specific date. I don't mind if it is after one year or two years," she ordered.

"But aunty, I think we are just friends," Samim said, scratching his head.

"What do mean by 'you think'?" she quizzed, frowned.

"I mean, she thinks we are just good friends. I have tried several times to tell her about my feelings, but I don't know..." Samim explained, disheartened. In the meanwhile, Dhritiman reached.

"You are hopeless. Ask her to marry you directly," she advised before walking to the car. Samim kept standing there, lost in thought. She returned to him and whispered, "There are lots of handsome guys in Delhi." He nodded helplessly. Ahi's parents left, after which Samim lit a cigarette, stepping out of the airport premises.

Formaldehyde, that famous preservative for cadavers in our anatomy laboratory and hospital, has an unpleasant odour. Many of my classmates felt nausea, headaches and ocular irritation that causes

tear overflow and a burning sensation in the throat because of that odour. However, I was comfortable as I had a habit of inhaling the smell of my own blood and flesh ever since my childhood.

The corpses were kept in zipped body-bags, tagged with their names. All those names definitely had been of some significance to other's lives and society before they were reduced to tags and turned to mere lab specimens.

I still remember how that scalpel blade in my shivering hand pierced skin the first time; it was messy. I had to peel only, but my rookie hand cut it deep to the muscle; blood splattered on my face and body. "This incision has to be straight. Don't cut too deep, otherwise, the muscles will be damaged. Just slice through the subcutaneous fat; easy there, carefully." The lab instructor sounded like a cold-blooded murderer.

Few weeks after the completion of our anatomy course, we held a ceremony to honour the sacrifices of those who had donated their bodies for our learning. Even those corpses were more fortunate than me; we accomplished their wishes even after their demise. On the other hand, I used to be punished even for nurturing any wish.

"Ma'am, could you please open your tray table?" An air-hostess requested. Ahi kept the manuscript aside and unfolded the tray.

"Your non-veg dinner," the air-hostess informed, placing the food on the tray.

Ahi's stomach rolled a warning as nausea gripped her, seeing the chicken pieces on her plate. She covered her mouth and ran to the restroom. She did not attempt to read the manuscript then, neither did she have dinner; the rest of her journey was spent in listening to Rabindra Sangeet.

Ahi easily found Jaideep uncle outside the arrival gate as she came out of the airport. That middle-aged, short businessman was not Ahi's uncle by any family or blood relation. During Dhritiman's posting in Noida, Jaideep was one of his neighbours and Dhritiman had helped him to set up his first business. He visited Dhritiman and his family whenever he came to Kolkata and stayed at their home. Gradually, he became family.

Initially, Ahi's mother was a bit reluctant regarding her daughter's stay with Jaideep as he was a bachelor who lived alone. But eventually, Dhritiman was able to convince his wife after several lengthy discussions.

"Look at you, my young lady!" he greeted Ahi, grinning and snatched the trolley from her.

"It… It's okay, uncle," Ahi fumbled, nervously.

"You are my guest now," Jaideep uncle said and started walking towards the parking. Ahi followed him. They reached Jaideep's apartment at sector twenty-six, Noida, almost after one hour. Ahi called her mother on the way just to get rid of the extremely talkative Jaideep; dealing with her hyper mother was preferable, comparatively.

Jaideep's two bedroom flat on the third floor seemed like a temporary shelter to Ahi. The apartment looked as if it had been arranged in a hurry with the basic necessities of life.

The flat was mostly empty, except one room which was contrastingly arranged with a king-size bed, full-length mirror, carpet on the floor, a wooden wardrobe and all kind of amenities.

"Princess, this is your room. If you need anything, just let your uncle know," Jaideep informed, dramatically leaning his head. Ahi smiled, hesitatingly. "And this is a duplicate key," he added.

Ill health, few sleep deprived nights and the exhaustion of the journey convinced Ahi to sleep early that night, against her wish to read a few more pages of that irresistible manuscript.

Ahi had been relishing the pleasant-sounding chorus of chanting and the temple bell which rather made her early morning's somnolent state, denser. After spending a few lethargic hours in bed, she woke up to find Jaideep uncle, placing a coffee mug and a biscuit packet on the small stool by her bed.

"Good morning Ahi! How are you feeling today?" he greeted and asked, marked by his signature grin.

"Much better than yesterday, uncle," Ahi replied yawning and stretching her arms.

"Your mother has been trying your mobile since morning; at last she called me. I will be back late at night; you just lock the door properly before sleeping. I have a spare key for myself," he informed and left the room hurriedly.

She stepped out of her bed, walked towards the open window, facing a mounted roof of a temple. The street in front of the temple was partly visible from that window. A tiny group of people were busy in constructing the marquee around the temple. She smiled, pleased to know that she was not going to miss Durga Puja.

Ahi always wanted to spend Durga Puja in Kolkata, tasting local foods like phuchka, kachori, biryani and other Bong delicacies; healthy dietary and fitness freak Ahi would transform into a contradictory avatar under the influence of a split-personality disorder on those days. She wanted to hang out all day long with her childhood friends at the local puja-marquee and to hop around the city in the evening from one pandal to another. However, her priorities and perceptions had changed gradually with her maturity; those small wishes seemed silly just as Tintin and Harry Potter gave way to other mature and realistic grey characters.

Ahi planned to visit Devang Awasthi's home that day, but it was too early to knock on some stranger's door at seven in the morning. Hence, she reached the terrace, carrying the manuscript, her coffee mug, mobile and cigarette packet. Every city looks so innocent, calm and peaceful at that time of the day. The dark clouds covered the sun at horizon, lengthening the duration of the dawn accompanied by the breeze. A handful of people were busy sweeping the streets while a few shopkeepers were engaged in their morning prayers, hoping their small businesses would make enough profit.

Ahi sat on a staircase leading to a smaller roof where a gigantic water-tank was placed, and started reading.

The coalesced odour of preservatives, blood, flesh, and urine from those cadavers resided in my nasal passages for years, completely seizing my olfaction; none of my expensive perfumes could defeat that odour of my nastiest nostalgia. However, the aroma of Sanjivani's cuisines had rejuvenated the entire passageway, starting from my nasal vestibule to the olfactory bulb of my brain. She was the magician of culinary art to play with the five sense organs of a human.

Eventually, Sanjivani had turned that oubliette of Master into a perfect home I had always dreamt about. Having a normal life must sound simple for others; as a matter of fact, it is a laid back achievable for many. However, normal life was undreamt-of concept to me before Sanjivani had stepped into my life. Her compassion and humanity were large enough to wrap all of our domestic help; unlike me, she could resonate their feelings and desires. They used to stand by our gigantic, twelve-seater dining table, waiting for Master's and my orders during breakfast, lunch, and dinner. She had just abolished all those rules, inviting them to share the dining with us. Initially, they were hesitant to obey, but they had to break the shackles of their slavish habits on her insistence. Those lit up faces in felicity, those harmonious giggles, and laughs had wiped out that eerie gloominess and silence of Master's dungeon.

After a couple of years, we were blessed with a baby boy. Aging was so satiating, counting those cumulative wrinkles on my face like my owned trophies through life's normal course of events like marriage, spending time with family, having kids and raising the posterity day-by-day.

Ahi, being a woman, was happy learning how Sanjivani had healed the author's disturbed life by her affection, love and humanity. The fluently flowing words, describing the good times of author's life kept Ahi's heart pleasurable; a trace of a pleasing smile was static on her face while she was perusing those pages until her phone rang.

"Haan Maa," Ahi responded.

"How are you feeling today? Had your medicines?" Ahi's mother began.

"No, I have not. I am feeling absolutely fresh and energetic."

"But still, you have to complete the course. Every medicine has a certain number of doses to be completed; otherwise, you will fall sick again. I will call you again in the evening to hear that you have had your medicines. Okay?" her mother admonished.

"Okay, Mother India, I will. Bye now, I have to do some work," Ahi assured to keep her calm.

Ahi felt a strange shudder of being watched by someone nearby as she attempted to get down from the staircase. She found a woman in reddish saree at a window of a dilapidated building, not very far from her. Ahi ran towards the nearest parapet to have a comparatively closer glimpse. However, she was quick to hide behind the wall.

A lmost after fifteen minutes of cycling, the rickshaw reached an enormous bungalow in sector nineteen.

"Madam ji, this is the house," the rickshaw-puller informed her, gripping the handbrake tightly.

Ahi paid the rickshaw-puller and walked towards the huge iron gate. That bungalow was surrounded by a tall stone-wall with only one opening, fenced by a large iron gate. That rusted iron-skeleton was fashioned in several artistic curves and tiny shapes which gave it an antique look, though the hinges were undoubtedly replaced recently to grip the whole structure firmly. Numerous vines had crept all over the wall. A wide panel, fastened on the wall next to the iron gate was struggling for its existence to bear the occupants' names of Awasthi Nivas – Devraj Awasthi and Devang Awasthi with their professions and endless degrees. The bungalow behind the wall and gate was connected through a narrow pathway, covered in different colours of pebbles, bisecting a widely-spread lawn. However, the lawn had lost its green, dried-out as yellowish white and often exposed the soil to the air. It seemed like an abandoned kingdom that was built with immense passion, enthusiasm, and attention by the king, but due to some maledictions, had lost all its vigour, emblazonment and attraction.

Ahi hesitantly pushed the gate, not finding any calling-bell around; it swung open, clanging. A chilled breeze blew on her. An eerie feeling that she was there to satiate someone's prolonged unfulfilled desire filled her with dread; her feet shook as she walked in. However, her obsession to publish that manuscript pushed her for a few more steps till she heard a voice which asked,

"Beti, who are you looking for?" She turned around to find a scrawny, short, aged and dark man; his head and face covered in uncombed grey hair. It was quite impossible to recognise his body, lost inside his oversized shirt and pyjama. It seemed his clothes were hanging in the air.

"Uncle, is anyone at home?" Ahi asked with a pleasant smile, identifying him as the domestic help.

"No one is at home now. But they will come back shortly. You can come inside and wait for some time," he suggested, stretching the wrinkles on his face by an elongated grin. Ahi nodded, smiling.

Ahi entered a giant drawing room on the ground floor, following the old man.

"Wait here," he requested, pointing to a semi-circular sofa, surrounding a centre table and vanished somewhere in that gigantic, mazy bungalow.

Ahi was amazed to find the striking similarities of that place with the minute and vivid detailing by Devang Awasthi in his manuscript to describe that place. She felt like a frequent visitor even though she was visiting the place for the first time. Eventually, her eyes encountered a closed door, the first on the left crossing the drawing room, the punishment room as defined in the manuscript. She reached in front of that closed door and pushed it open to enter the room. Yes, she found that twin effortlessly in that room what her eyes were craving for, two white walls facing each other, holding two large portraits on their chests. The woman on one of those portraits was just a human imitation of the goddess. Ahi gazed at her in amazement for a while before turning to the other wall where the portrait of Devaraj Awasthi was fastened. The decent and gallant man of the picture in a black suit and precisely knitted red tie, had his black hair perfectly combed and partitioned on the left-side. His thick moustache was neatly trimmed above his upper lip; the deep pair of eyes were covered beneath the thick glasses of spectacle. Ahi found the superfluous calmness on his face inhuman; must be to disguise his aggression and maliciousness from society. Ahi pawed that mute witness of those brutal incidents, that white wall beneath the portrait; her vision blurred with tears. All of a sudden, her attention went on the wooden floor as she felt something sticky under her feet. She lifted her feet to find blood under her feet. She kneeled down on the floor to find few tinier blood-puddles and drops making a trail, leading towards the widest corner of the room. Ahi's ears and nose-tip turned red in fright; she felt palpitation under her rib-cage. She was shivering as her eyes followed that blood-trail to find a pair of bare, trembling feet, trying hard to crimp all the fingers together. The blood was dripping on the feet, rolling over the thighs and knees. Ahi started slowly moving her eyes upwards to see the face. But that pair of legs evaporated along with the splattered blood on the floor while she heard a modulated female voice, asking "May I know, who are you?" and she turned around to respond.

Ahi stumbled over her own crossed feet and fell down as she tried to stand hastily.

"Hi… Hi Ma'am, I am A… Ahi from Ankur Publication; wanted to discuss a manuscript which has reached our office for editorial evaluation and publishing," Ahi replied fumbling, followed by a moronic grin to cover up her imprudent act.

The fair and tall woman in a sports bra, shorts, and running shoes gazed at Ahi for a few moments from head to toe. The gliding drops of sweat on her skin and the white towel wrapped around her neck made her extensive workout session obvious to Ahi. She had an awkward skin-and-bone structure, similar to her artificially sophisticated face; as if she was arrogantly chasing her age to draw it back in a stalemate. She was skinny and her cheek bones just gave her a skeletal look.

"Wow! Impressive," she responded snorting while mopping her face with the towel. "Excuse…" she uttered, making a sullen face. Ahi was quite shocked by her misbehaviour.

"Actually, it is not an… excuse," Ahi imitated her talking-tempo as she replied, leaving a mute moment before voicing the word 'excuse'. "In fact, I have the manuscript with me," Ahi added, pulling out the bunch of papers from her bag.

"Hello! Miss whoever you are… you are standing in my home," she almost threatened Ahi in a modulated tone, concealing her seething anger at Ahi's mockery. "I don't give a damn about all his writing and stuff. I just threw off all his crap after his death. By the way, I like my guest to behave like a guest and sit decently in the drawing room; not snoop around with some rehearsed and lame excuse. What are you looking for in this room?" she continued, almost leaning into Ahi's face with a frown.

Ahi ran out of words. In the meanwhile, that old man in oversized clothes arrived carrying a tea-tray.

"Hari, where were you?" the skinny woman screamed at the top of her voice, rushing towards him like a tigress hunts her prey in hunger. "Who opened this room? How did she enter this room?" she darted her questions one after the other.

Ahi was standing like a mute witness wondering what would hurt more: swallowing a bit of humiliation from this cranky woman or returning to Kolkata empty-handed.

"Dusting *ke liye*, Madam," he mumbled, gathering courage.

"Shut up!" she shrieked. "How many times should I tell you that you don't need to do anything in this room and always keep this room closed," she admonished in a low voice, emphasising each word and gnashing her teeth. She left that place abruptly and hopped up the staircase in a hurry.

"I am sorry, uncle," Ahi consoled that old man with a smile, caressing his shoulder. He smiled back.

"I know where you are coming from. Just let him know that I have my eyes on him and I will definitely make him pay for this nonsense," that self-obsessed woman shouted back from the staircase, just before vanishing into a room upstairs. Ahi kept gazing in her direction. She brooded over all those bizarre incidents that had happened in the last few days since she had received that manuscript: that stalking woman, the man this zero-figure lady was talking about, and last but not the least, this woman herself. Why was she behaving in such a weird manner? She couldn't be Sanjivani. Then who was she?

"Beti, your tea is getting cold," the old man interrupted Ahi's virtual maze-walk as he placed the tea-tray on the centre table.

"Thank a lot for the tea, uncle. But I believe it is better for me to leave. I am sorry, but it is really sweet of you," Ahi apologised with a token of appreciation.

"Dear, all the guests of this house have always asked me to refill their cups after they finish the first cup and they consider my tea, refreshing and lucky for them. Have it, you will soon get whatever you are looking for," that old man offered with an affectionate smile on his face. Ahi could not turn him down.

Disappointed, Ahi returned to Jaideep's place in a confused state of mind; she was not prepared to face such adversity. On many such occasions in the past, Samim had helped her. He was the only person who she could trust in any situation. She pulled out her mobile to call Samim, but kept it back on second thoughts as he would be busy. The chorus of chanting and the temple bell drew all her attention as she attempted to enter the apartment.

The afternoon prayer just had finished when she reached there. A handful of people gathered for puja in front of a small Kaali idol inside the main temple. An unfinished Durga idol was kept aside under a temporarily constructed tent. It was a small, traditional, single-structured idol where Durga, her children, their mounts along with Mahishasur formed a single idol, connected to each other.

Ahi walked across the tiny ground in front of the temple to reach the main temple.

"Please help me. I have to publish this manuscript. Please! Please! Please help me! I will stop smoking; promise," Ahi prayed with closed eyes with an obeisance gesture of gathering her palms together.

The inevitable flow of times and Sanjivani's companionship had been healing my psychological wounds; physical wounds had left me as well, leaving those benign scars on my body. I had created several rejuvenating memories with my family. Those memories of playing hide-and-seek with my son, his chuckling, observing me struggling to find him after hiding behind the same curtain every time, those long discussions with Sanjivani after dinner over a glass of wine – pleasant, peaceful and impeccable. When I say time, time is not what we see on a mechanical or sun clock; they are just devices to measure the time. Time is not hours, minutes or seconds as well; they are just units to measure the time. Time is the continuous psychological and physical change within us, inevitable and unstoppable. However, that could not change my core.

Unlike Master, I had been raising my son with affection and care; moreover, he was blessed with the best possible mother, Sanjivani. But in all other aspects of my life, I was just a successor of my Master's footsteps. Spontaneously, I had never repented for the brutality. In fact, remorse, affection, love, benignity, and adherence were just a few impractical words for my intellection, action, and ideology. I know, it might sound like a self-contradictory statement, but it was not. My faultless paternity was my silent protest against Master; an escape-design from the psychic trauma of my puerility. And Sanjivani, yes, she was the love of my life, but more than that, I owed a lot to her. That thought gradually transformed my love into compensation.

I might have inherited that venomous seed inside my core from the Master; his poison was flowing through my veins, heart, brain and in each tissue of my body. Otherwise, how could I do that? It was not me; that venomous phantom who had been ruling my cerebration.

That incident is still vivid in my memory; how can I forget her face? Her corpse was placed on a stretcher in front me, under the surgical light as I entered the morgue. Morgue, the gloomy, chilled, motionless and silent waiting room for the cadavers; some of them were waiting for their relatives and family, hoping for the last respect, affection, and love before burial or cremation. However, few of those cadavers were not so fortunate because they had to wait for justice and their identification; she was one of them. Asha, a seventeen-year-old girl and daughter of a proud teacher. She had two elder brothers but that teacher had all his faith on that little girl to uphold his name in society.

Unlike others, that silent morgue was the noisiest and most distressing place for me because a corpse talks much more than a living human. And unlike a human, they always speak the truth. Asha's dead body was screaming for justice in front of me; her body was like an eloquent canvas, revealing a heinous painting on it.

She ran, ran like she had stolen her own life from them and they chased her to snatch it back. One of them tugged her scarf from behind to stop her, but she lost her balance due to her pace. She toppled over the ground to fracture the back of her head; the muddy blood over her occipital bone vividly visualised that. The blood clot on her throat had few sharp and deep scars; she must be wearing a synthetic scarf on that day. She skidded into a drowsy state; she felt the odour of alcohol from those leaning faces closed to hers, but her vision was blurred due to the vicious strike on her head. She was brave, brave enough to fight for her pride, even in that fragile physical condition. She scratched out the skin along with a bit of flesh of one among them; those skin-cells and bleeding pieces of flesh, tucked inside her nails were more than sufficient to thrash that particular man behind prison. They left their fingerprints all over her torso, along with mud, sand particles, bruises, and bite-marks of multiple sizes, which were more congested and bloodier over her breast. I could visualize their brutal dictatorship and insaneness of lust. Lust and revenge are the two strongest emotions of humans. Camouflage fails there. The bruises on her labia minora, hymenal rips at five and seven o'clock positions were oozing with blood, with a tear of the posterior fourchette … evidence enough that she was brutally raped. Finally, she had died due to excessive bleeding and incessant sexual assault.

However, I was paid a huge amount to act blind to all those obvious evidence; half of the amount had already been transferred to my bank account and the other half was about to be deposited after submitting my fake autopsy report to the court. That rape and murder case had reached a stalemate, waiting for my autopsy report; the three accused men were out on bail. I had two options in front of me – one was worse and another one was absolutely ugly. Hence, I had decided to choose the worse, submitting my fake report to the court and donating that amount to Asha's family. After all, that was their money, the trading price of Asha's pride. I too had my own interest behind that. Self-preservation – one of the basic motives of a human being.

One of those three accused rapists was the son of the coeval godfather of the entire national capital region. His father was a resolution of all problems for the politicians, industrialists or any other rich person who could pay his service charges. His services were especially those crimes which a decently masked kingpin of society cannot do to preserve their business of faking innocent people. He had arrived at my home one night, two days before the submission date of my report. His tall, wide and the severely suntanned body was covered with a milky white khadi kurta-pyjama. A few scars defaced his cheeks, a dense moustache and beard made his face fearsome; a perfect example of ugliness. I am sure he was satiated to see the fright in others' eyes.

"Good evening doctor," he greeted in his shrill voice, bribing me with a fifty-year-old bottle of Dalmore Decanter.

"Please," I requested him to sit, pointing to one of the chairs in the drawing room.

"Sure, but only after my son walks out free from all charges," he replied, carefully whiffing a bidi.

"What if I deny your request?"

He kept laughing insanely for a couple of minutes, then said, "You are not so stupid doctor." I didn't respond.

"Lots of bitches like her die in our country every day; it is just an addition to that. But, I don't want to lose the best doctor of our city; never. Doctor, he is my son; you can rob me, but cannot deny me this," he threatened, protruding his eyeballs before walking towards the exit. I was left standing there like a mannequin.

He turned back before stepping out of the door and said, "Pot calling the kettle black." He started laughing again as he marched out of the door.

My life seemed more expensive to me than dead Asha's pride. He would have killed her father and brothers too if I would have protested. Hence, I had decided to kill Asha once again after her death.

I noticed those moist and destitute eyes of Asha's father in the court while the judge was announcing the autopsy report. They collided with my eyes a few times to leave me ashamed momentarily. However, his mature calmness, occupied with a great deal of life experience was supporting my decision. He was well acquainted with the fact that he was not the fittest to fight against the system, which was made by the fittest, for the fittest. Her brothers were glowering at me. Their facial expressions made it easy for me to read their mind – inexperienced, alien to the reality and influenced by those fake fairy tales of heroism.

I knew that they would not directly accept the money. Hence, I summoned one of the men to meet Asha's father in disguise of his student's father and to leave behind the money at his home.

Ahi kept the manuscript aside, disturbed, seething and shattered at the same time. She fumbled to tap the cigarette between her lips before gasping a lung full of smoke, weeping. The visualization of Asha's dead body was haunting her. She wondered what initiation the police department had taken for justice; her father would have never allowed that catastrophe to take place. She simpered as her mobile rang. However, she responded, "Yes, Samim," promptly as Samim's name popped up on the screen.

"What happened? Are you okay? Is everything alright?" he asked in one breath, guessing something was wrong from Ahi's nasal voice due to her crying.

"I am not fine. I don't know what to do now. I am completely clueless, Samim. You guys are working so hard for the Puja-edition and I am just wasting my time here. I am so frustrated… huh," Ahi nagged like a maudlin kid, hearing Samim's voice. She was driven by her conviction that a problem is resolved if Samim hears it.

"Slow baby, slow! What happened, tell me in detail," Samim asked calmly in confidence of his experience of steering Ahi and her problems on many past occasions. Ahi described the course of events of the day in detail.

"Who was that lady, by the way?" Samim quizzed.

"I have no idea who is she, what is her relationship with Devang Awasthi and why the hell she was behaving so weirdly with a stranger," Ahi responded, sighing. After a few mute moments, she started fumbling, "I should have asked that old man. Oh shit! I shouldn't have lost my temper."

"Ahi, don't worry. There must be other family members. We just need the signature of any one of them – his wife, son, daughter, brother, whoever will work for us," Samim encouraged.

"Yes, I have to do something."

"By the way, Pranab da is not missing any tiny chance to make a fuss about your travel to Noida," Samim informed.

"Oh god! I knew it." Ahi was concerned.

Their discussion continued, not giving Samim a chance to speak his heart out and propose to Ahi.

Another day had passed. Ahi did not get a breakthrough even after wandering around Awasthi Nivas quite a few times; rather she attracted the unnecessary attention of some random passersby. She had not seen anyone other than that cranky lady coming out or going inside the bungalow. Having no alternatives, she returned to Jaideep's flat in the evening, dismayed. She decided to go back to Kolkata the next morning. Unfortunately, there were tickets only for the day after. She called her mother and Samim to inform them about the same. However, she was unaware of the surprises and shocks which her fate had designed to turn her life upside down in the days to come.

Later she picked up the manuscript addictively from the bed and started reading.

I was sustaining in that dark world, inherited from Master; once one had been introduced to that world, there was no back alley to return to, except death. Master not only introduced me to that world, he enrooted me. I was acquainted of all those illegal businesses, the masterminds, the touts and the entire network which had been operating that empire. Trade of human organs and selling infants to the rich and infertile couples were the most profitable among those illegal businesses. However, I had never felt any remorse. No business can flourish without its demands; it was our own hypocritical society which was nourishing that bootleg market.

I had never forgotten to wear the human skin before returning home from work only to keep Sanjivani and my son Dhruv, incognisant of my real face. But the truth is irreversible and impossible to conceal. One day, my mask fell apart when the police arrived at my home to interrogate me, a few months after Asha's death; her brothers had apparently filed a complaint. Though their charges could not survive more than a few weeks as her brothers also got to meet that rapist's father. However, that incident planted a seed of suspicion in Sanjivani's mind.

Empathy, the ability to comprehend and share other's emotional state, originates from the anterior insular cortex of our brain and a few of us have this ability way stronger than usual. To my luck, Sanjivani was one of them. Any news of mishap or accident on television always triggered tears in her eyes. She had always been concerned about the education, nourishment, health, and well-being of the kids of our housemaids, driver, gardener, milkman and other comparatively financially weaker people around us. She had never hesitated for a second to give away herself completely to see a smile on their faces. On many occasions, she had emptied her purse for some beggar on the street and had brought home those kids who were begging on the street. I had never opposed her because that heart of gold and these actions were the essence of Sanjivani; the woman with a treasured and rare heart.

I encouraged her to start a charitable organization to help those deprived of all basic needs to survive, especially children. She accepted. I did notice a magical glow on her face as if she had found the true meaning of her life. Neither was I the person to play the game of winning brownie points with god to dissolve my sins, nor was I as sympathetic as Sanjivani. I helped her to set up her charitable organization to divert her attention from me. But it turned into a backlash. She firmly bellieved that her work was incomplete while her husband might be the reason for someone's misery. She started spying on me, considering that as her job. Eventually, my disguise completely fell apart as she found some evidence. She stopped talking to me, as if she had undertaken a vow of reticence. Not for a day or a few weeks, but months. She was numb with shock. I know she had been waiting for my explanation in self-defence which could satisfy her senses about my innocence. However, I was acquainted of my justification, and it was not saleable to her. Hence, I kept waiting for her to recover from that disquieted state of mind, forgetting everything. I was wrong. Time did not heal that wound in her heart, and the silence eventually compelled her to outdistance me forever.

Sanjivani's love for me was unadulterated, an unconditional selflessness, and it shackled her to pursue any action against me. On the contrary, her compassion had been weeping silently to her consciousness for justice. That surreptitious war in her mind had split her soul into two parts. In medical terms, it was bipolar disorder. She had been suffering from depression and frequent mood swings. Though we all go through these kinds of emotional ups and downs in our daily courses of life, but for a person with bipolar disorder, these peaks and ditches are sharp and extremely contrasting. It affected her energy state, the ability of judgment, concentration, memory, appetite, sleep patterns, sex drive, and self-esteem. Additionally, bipolar disorder had cursed her in the form of anxiety, substance abuse, and health problems such as diabetes, heart disease, migraines, and high blood pressure. She went through rigorous counselling sessions for a long period of almost five years, but her health did not improve even a trifle. Mental disorders cannot be cured until the impacted mind is willing to be healed. It seemed like Sanjivani had decided to live a dormant life to escape from her senses, which had been pricking her soul, reminding her of me, her killer husband.

Her condition deteriorated with every passing second. One day she attempted to kill one of the maids by stabbing her with a fork and then tried to commit suicide in remorse. Her psychiatrist advised us to admit her in an asylum. However, I preferred to keep her restricted at home itself and summoned a nurse to take care of her in my absence. It was getting from bad to worse with the passage of time, and sometimes, I had to shackle her to refrain her from any further harm. She had been dying every moment since then. Each of those days, she used to do something terribly wrong, contrary to her character, in depression.

She did not deserve that life, I knew, and only aconite could provide Sanjivani the peace she needed badly. It would also secure my self-preservation as aconite doesn't leave any symptom of poisoning that an autopsy can capture. Aconite is like a con artist who enter our lives in the disguise of a lover, friend, well-wisher, or sympathiser to exploit our confidence, emotions and even our survival instinct, later vanishes abruptly, leaving no trace behind, other than an invisible and fatal wound in our minds and hearts. It is readily available in the Indian market in the form of dried shrivelled root of the plant monkshood, also known as devil's helmet. It first stimulates the sensory and motor nerves to paralyze them, then it attacks the exchange of oxygen and carbon dioxide, chocking the ventilation of lungs, which causes an arrhythmic heart function and suffocation. Just thirty minutes of tolerance would gift eternal peace and escape from all the pains of life.

"Fucking no way, please," Ahi pleaded, whispering and flipping the page in a hurry.

That day, I released that nurse a little early after returning home from the hospital, and prepared Sanjivani's favourite drink – my signature hand-made beaten coffee. She used to love it, especially whenever I prepared it. That dust of peace, the crushed root of aconite, was smoothly mixed in that drink.

She was sleeping in peace, basking in the softness and warmth of the bed while I entered the room, carrying the coffee mug. Yes, she needed that peace. Her face had a stillness like the soft sun rays, sparkling on the vivid and recently water-washed greenery after a horrific storm. I kept the mug on a small table by her bed, pulled a chair for myself and lounged close to the bed. I kept gazing at her calm and innocent face for several minutes.

"Oh, you should have woken me up. How long were you waiting for me?" Sanjivani whispered in a sleepy voice, pushing herself on the bed in an attempt to sit straight.

"How are you feeling now?" I asked, leaving the chair and sitting on the bed next to her. She nodded, hiding her face on my chest. I

kissed her forehead, embracing her tightly in my arms for the last time. She started weeping, inconsolably, as I caressed her face.

"See, I have prepared your favourite beaten coffee," I tried to make her smile for the last time, picking the coffee mug from the table. She held the mug like a kid, a satisfactory smile on her face and tears in her eyes.

"Sanju, this coffee will give you freedom from all this pain," I whispered.

She had developed a sense of reading unspoken words, comprehending the minutest of facial expressions through the experiences of her nursing career. After all, she had to take care of many patients who had lost their ability to speak and could express nothing but mere, minute facial expressions. For a second, I felt that she knew my intention as she looked straight into my eyes after a sip of that coffee. However, neither did she refuse to drink it, nor did she protest. Rather, she said, "Take care of Dhruv," and placed her palm on my face.

Her lips, tongue and throat tingled, followed by salivation after a few sips. She did not stop sipping the coffee until it spilled on the bed as she was panting heavily. I held her tightly in my arms. Yes, that was the first time I felt remorse and grief for a moment. For the first time, my eyes were moist in emotion. She fidgeted for a few minutes, moaning; numbness followed in her limbs first, then in her torso. Tears oozed out of the corners of my eyes. She collapsed in my arms. I could sense that her irregular heartbeats were giving up slowly, and finally stopped after some time.

I committed the crime under the influence of the most complex emotion of the human mind, love, which was derived from kindness in my case. Love, the only human emotion which is both primitive and composite. In some occasions, other emotions such as desire, lust, addiction, kindness, affection and even hate derive from love, and in other events of life, love oozes from need, habit, trust, indulgence,

respect and many other essences of life. This deceptively simple word
of four letters is the most complex emotion. Scientifically, it is a
special state of mind, which takes only one-fifth of a second for the
euphoria along with the chemicals to start to impact the brain when
we look at that special someone; twelve different areas of our brain
are the culprits for this mental chaos. When we see or think about
that special person, these areas release a cocktail of neurotransmitters
across the brain, together with oxytocin, dopamine, vasopressin,
and adrenaline.

"I knew it; that ill-tempered lady couldn't have been Sanjivani,"
Ahi muttered to herself. She threw the manuscript away and hid
her face behind a pillow, disturbed and hurt.

Ahi felt an unbearable pain in her neck as she woke up the next
morning; she had fallen asleep in a bad position. The tiredness
of the past few sleep-deprived nights became stronger.

"Ahh!" she cried out as she moved her head to grab the cigarette
packet on the bed.

Her eyebrows, lips, cheekbones, and jaws were manifesting a
sappy emotion while she was blowing those smoke-rings through her
puckered lips, broodingly. Happiness tinged her thoughts as she could
attend Durga Puja back in Kolkata. But she was more upset about
the missed opportunity for herself and her publication house, Ankur.

Eventually, her eyes fell on a scrunched paper ball on the floor;
she wondered where that came from as she could not remember

throwing that on the floor. She picked up the paper ball in curiosity, getting out of the bed. It was quite heavy for paper. She flattened the paper to find a stone wrapped inside. Not finding anything suspicious after scrutinizing the stone, she kept it on the table. Someone must have used the stone to throw the paper to me, she thought. She read those printed lines on that shady, furrowed paper –

I have keys, but no locks. I have space, but no rooms. I am an unsung hero in modern days; because my famous brother had replaced me from your desk. However, I taught him everything he knows. Can you forget the nostalgia of those letters, pressing my ribbon of ink? Reach the address below to meet me.

An address of a scrap dealer was written below the note. "What the fuck is this?" Ahi whispered to herself. After gazing at that piece paper for some time, she detected something weird. She picked the manuscript from her bed, kept it on the table and placed the piece of paper on the manuscript.

"This is fucking bizarre," she whispered to find the same broken 'T' and 'S' in both the places. She captured an image of it in her mobile and sent it to Samim. Her phone rang immediately after the picture had delivered.

"Samim, what the hell does this mean?" Ahi quizzed, receiving the call.

"Don't you think I should ask that question?" Samim asked.

"I have no idea. I found this piece of paper on the floor after waking up. If you could figure out the meaning of it..." Ahi said, smashing the filter in the ashtray.

"It looks like a riddle; just ignore it, whatever it is. By the way, have you done your packing or not?" Samim asked, evading her question.

"Not yet, I will do it in the evening," she answered. Her demoralized voice conveyed her disappointment to Samim.

"Hey, do you know the government is planning a long procession this year of all the Durga idols of Kolkata for immersion together. Just imagine the colours and lights; it is going to be the biggest carnival ever in India," Samim attempted to cheer her up, as usual. He hated to see Ahi troubled. If possible, he was ready to become a clown for his entire life just to light Ahi's face with a smile. But, he failed this time.

"Samim, I will call you back in the evening," Ahi assured before hanging up.

Several waves of doubts swept over Ahi's mind while she was filling up her first coffee mug of the day. But those waves were dispelling at the cost of her own reasoning. Someone was using the same typewriter that had been used to type that manuscript. She wondered whether Devang Awasthi was still alive and wanted to publish his autobiography. Then what about the media coverage of his death; were they all fake? Why did he do that? Why did he have to choose a small publisher like Ankur for that? What might be the meaning of those lines and why had she been chosen?

Should she visit the place mentioned on that paper? Would it be safe for her, she wondered. Anyway, what could go wrong in broad daylight? she smirked. She poured the rest of the coffee into the sink, freshened up quickly and headed out. A morbid curiosity got the better of her and she left in the same clothes that she had worn the previous night; pair of shorts and vest top.

Atta market, the sector eighteen market of Noida, is famous for its never-ending assortments of small shops of cheap apparel, footwear, plastic items, garments, provisions and other home supplies. Mocking Noida's largest shopping mall, The Great Indian Place on the other end of the road, Atta market has been growing their old traditional business vigorously; the mecca for buyers to hone their bargaining skills. The shopkeepers also demonstrate their expertise in inducing their customers with their surprising concessions on overpriced items; they win the deal behind the drape, pretending to be defeated by their clients.

When Ahi reached the address of the scrap dealer, most of the shops were closed and the street was not too crowded. She found the place after wandering for a few minutes. looking at those sideboards fastened over each shop. Ahi was uncomfortable as her attire was catching everyone's eyes on the street. Even the teenaged boy at that scrap-shop was not an exception.

"*Kya chahiye, didi?*" he asked, gazing at her widely-exposed cleavage.

"Is this the address of this shop?" Ahi asked holding that piece of paper in front of that lad. He glanced at it reluctantly, moving his eyes from Ahi, and nodded confirming. On an impulse, Ahi thought of asking that boy whether he or someone from that shop had thrown the paper. But, soon she realized that the English riddle would be beyond his capacity.

"Do you want to meet my uncle?" he quizzed, a tad bit impatiently. Ahi made a footling gesture, nodding to buy some time to hang around there. The boy gestured to her to sit on a bench inside the shop and flew out of the shop in a hurry. The shop was stuffed with scrapped metal, rods, plastic, heaps of paper, broken furniture, electronic gadgets and various other things Ahi would simply call garbage. Ahi was sitting there in quandary between sating her curiosity over the piece of paper or leaving the place abruptly. In the meanwhile, that boy returned carrying two glasses of tea and offered one to Ahi. She grabbed the glass, smiling; the boy smiled back.

It might be a typewriter. A message popped up on the screen as Ahi unlocked her mobile in response to the message tone. Samim had come to the rescue again. She replied, *I love you.*

"Do you have a typewriter?" Ahi asked that boy, boiling in enthusiasm. The boy vanished, running away through that narrow alley between heaps of scraps, not answering her.

"What the fuck?" she whispered to herself, perplexed.

A few men were assembled at a street-side stall in front the shop. Ahi's eyes encountered the eyes of one of them as she looked at the road hearing the noise outside.

"Abey, look at that item!" that man goaded his companions.

Ahi turned her face away from them as she became the centre of attention of that rambunctious group. Meanwhile, that boy returned, careening to carry a heavy typewriter in his scrawny hands. Somehow, he managed to place it on the bench.

"We have two typewriters, one is completely broken and this one. Someone has sold this to us a few days back," the boy informed flamboyantly, observing the pleasing glow on Ahi's face.

"Chhotu, can you get me some paper," Ahi requested. The boy tore apart a sheet from an old notepad and rendered it to Ahi.

He stood close to her, gazing at the typewriter spellbindingly. He could not miss that opportunity to satiate his long-time curiosity about that instrument.

"What will you do with that typewriter? Baby, it will hurt your soft fingers. Rather, use my pen, full of white ink. If you wish, I can write a new story of your life with that," one of those men beleaguered; others burst into laughter. Ahi ignored them, conscious of the fact that her attire was garnering the unwanted attention.

She managed to place the sheet between the paper table and roller of that typewriter, turned the knob to feed the paper into the roller until the top of the paper was adjusted behind the key and moved the carriage to the left-most position on the sheet.

"Baby, please twist my roller also," another man teased. Ahi glowered at him.

Ahi typed 'I had never forgotten to wear that human skin before returning home from work, only to keep Sanjivani and my son, Dhruv incognisant of my real face' on that sheet.

She smiled as she found the exact same broken 'T' and 'S' in her typed sentence as in Devang Awasthi's manuscript. However, that glow turned into gloominess as those men entered the shop. One of them sat on the bench close behind her and others stood surrounding her. She felt his warm breath on her bare shoulder.

"*Oye chirkut, chal futle,*" one of them ordered, pushing the boy down on the floor, asking him to get lost. He stood up hastily and ran out of the shop to call his uncle.

Another man attempted to take down the shutter of the shop, but something thrashed him violently on the floor before he could close it completely. A more than six feet tall and wide, gigantic silhouette darkened by the bright sunlight outside, entered the shop, violently pushing up the shutter with a loud clanging sound. Two more silhouettes followed the first. Eventually, she could see it was a group of three transgenders. Their long nails were polished red, wrists were covered in bangles, buns at the back of their heads were decorated with wreaths, and lips were covered with a thick layer of lipstick.

"Get lost kids," the mammoth leader of that group of transgenders ordered and tucked her sunglasses into her blouse.

The man who sat on the bench sprung up and rushed to those intruders, toughening his fist. He threw a punch gathering all his strength, but she grabbed it effortlessly by the left hand and her muscular right hand punched his face consecutively three times to fracture his nose and lips; blood started dripping from his face. The other men ran away from there, scared witnessing their leader's condition. The wounded man also followed them, covering his face to stop the bleeding.

"*Hai hai! Yeh toh sach main pari hai re,*" one of them exclaimed in bliss, followed by their signature applauses. The leader came close to Ahi, sat on her toes in front of her and caressed Ahi's face affectionately. Ahi's eyes were glued on her moist eyes till they left abruptly after a few moments.

Soon after, that boy reached the shop along with his uncle, panting heavily, and started quizzing Ahi. She tactfully evaded all of their questions and left the shop, purchasing the typewriter from them.

The incident completely shook Ahi. She was scared, nervous and perplexed. She locked herself inside the restroom once she reached Jaideep's flat and stood under the shower for quite a long time, until her heartbeat pacified.

After debating the entire day whether to leave or chase the accomplishment of publishing the manuscript, Ahi finally decided to cancel her flight ticket and informed her mother and Samim about her extended stay. Ahi had to put in immense effort to convince her mother, but was finally able to.

She had no doubt that the message was for her and someone was out there to either help her or trap her. After all, her father had made plenty of enemies, thanks to his job. Moreover, who could be the kryptonite other than Ahi to destroy Dhritiman's life forever. She wondered whether that manuscript was just a bait to bring her out of Dhritiman's territory – Kolkata.

An urge had been spurring her to meet Hari, the servant of Awasthi Nivas, to get that typewriter identified as Devang Awasthi's. Hari's unanimity could equip Ahi to convince that self-obsessed, grumpy lady to sign the agreement on behalf of the author, even though Ahi was not certain about her relation with Devang Awasthi. Ahi wondered whether Hari could help her. She slipped into a pair of jeans and full-sleeved shirt. However, the phobia of that morning's incident diminished her courage to step out. After several meanderings inside that empty flat, she settled on the bed and decided to read the manuscript.

Euthanasia or mercy-killing, the practice of intentionally ending a life to relieve pain and suffering. Jurisdictions of few countries like Netherlands, Canada, Colombia, Belgium, and Luxembourg consider voluntary euthanasia as a legal act. In some other countries, voluntary euthanasia is still a divisible controversy from the perception of morality, humanity, ethics and religious beliefs. Anyway, involuntary euthanasia which is performed without asking for a patient's consent or against the patient's will is still illegal in all countries. However, what if a patient is in a coma or disabled in judging right or wrong. Should they be left to suffer and face death every day till their natural death? I could not bear that.

Which is illegal today, our need tomorrow, other's business a day after and rule after few days – that is how the human revolution works.

That giggle, laugh, and chin-wag which had resonated the waves of happiness in my home, the hustle and bustle from morning to night, those small talks which we used to share at the dining table, the efforts to put a smile on everyone's face, had vanished after Sanjivani's demise. I released all my domestic help, except my chauffeur and cook. Few years had passed after that incident, but it had never faded out from my mind; it always haunted me. I had immersed myself in my businesses, precisely in the illegal and brutal parts of it, hoping to commit a sin which could wipe out that new and extraneous feeling – the remorse of killing Sanjivani.

Dhruv had been growing up like those neglected weeds which crowd out the cultivated plants of a garden – desperate, uncultured, destructive, ruthless and unproductive. From early days of his age, he had comprehended the fact that his father was one of the richest persons of the city. Law and order were just jokes for him as he knew his father could conciliate all his boisterous activities, whatever and howsoever serious it could be. He had a few spineless friends around him to exploit his rich, ingrained and mighty background. He started stuffing drugs in his veins when he was only fifteen years old; cigarettes, marijuana and alcohol were naive stuff.

Though Master was a brutal monster inside the walls of my home, he was a successful father outside them. I had miserably failed to defeat him in that department.

Sisyphean, the word which can perfectly describe my life then, originated from Greek mythology. According to Greek mythology, Sisyphus was the king of Ephyra, well known as Corinth in present days. The king was cursed and punished for his self-aggrandizing craftiness; he was forced to roll an immense rock up to the top of a hill, only to tolerate the pain when that colossal boulder avalanched and hit him brutally, repeating that action for eternity.

I had two gigantic stones in my Sisyphean life, defeating Master as a father in raising Dhruv and abolishing the remorse of killing Sanjivani from my mind. My cursed, shackled and futile life got a pair of wings after a few more years when Radha stepped into my life. She was appointed as our cook, recommended by my driver. My life was much chaotic and complex to be concerned about trifling stuff. Hence, I let my chauffeur to take up all the responsibilities of her accommodation in that small outhouse at the back of our bungalow and teach her about our food habits and timings as well.

Few months had passed since she started working in my home, but I had completely forgotten her as I used to spend most of my time at different workplaces. I had not even seen her until that eventful night. That night, I had returned home a little early compared to other days with an intention to complete one of my novels. An inner strife which had been popping up in my mind for the last few days then about the climax of that particular novel, reached a conclusion that night. My fingers were busy on the keys of my typewriter to knit my thoughts on paper. The tapping sounds of the keys, the 'ding' while making a new line and that typical sound of rotating the roller had always acted like enchanted spells which smoothened the flows of words in my mind. All of a sudden, my fingers stopped as the consequence of an impulse reaction. I heard a male voice, faint in magnitude but lurid in attribute. It was coming from the outhouse. The scream was not loud enough to conquer the shield of closed doors and windows, but the tone was eloquent enough to manifest the anger and extreme nastiness.

I had to abandon my writing desk in a hurry. I was determined to teach Dhruv a lesson as I hurried through the stairs to reach the ground floor. I was exhausted and frustrated, tolerating his raucousness on daily basis. The voice was becoming louder as I was approaching the exact spot. The language was vulgar. I doubted the voice was Dhruv's. However, I reached the backyard almost running down the alleyway through the lawn as I was worried about our new cook, Radha.

Initially, I could not find anyone other than a tall and skinny man in a lungi and shirt, facing the wall. His hands were busy pushing something violently against the wall. Though it was impossible to *identify him in that darkness, I was quite sure that I had not seen that man before in my life.*

"Saali! Randi, aaj kaun bachaega tujhe?" that man grumbled, panting heavily to increase the thrust on the wall. His legs slipped backward on the muddy ground as he tried to gain more strength.

"What's going on here?" I asked loudly.

He turned back to me and hollered, "Benchod, who are you?" A lady in saree collapsed on the ground as soon as he moved away from the wall. I guessed it was Radha.

The man approached me, limping. His bulged out, red pair of eyes glued to me. He had messy hair like a nest of a bird on his skinny, haphazardly wrinkled and suntanned face.

"She is my wife. I have the right to do anything with her," he said, tilting his face close to mine. His odour could be used as an alternative anaesthesia on any normal human unlike me. The smell of concentrated sweat and grime on his body blended with the odour of cheap alcohol.

"I don't care who you are and I don't want to involve in any of your personal matter as well. But this is my house and I won't tolerate any kind of nonsense here. So, get the hell out of here. Otherwise I have to call the police," I admonished calmly.

He kept gazing at me. I had encountered those kind of eyes several times in my life; fearless, desperate and self-destructive. The weakness was their source of strength as they had nothing to lose anymore.

"I should call the police, not you. Have you taken my permission to keep my wife at your home?" He retorted, grabbing my collar. I shook his hand off hastily and pushed him back. He was too drunk to keep

his feet firm and fell down on the ground. His few failed attempts to get up on his feet angered him further. I had to call my chauffeur to take him outside my home and take care of Radha, though she got her consciousness back in the meanwhile. She was standing in a corner, hiding her face in her saree, petrified.

Next morning, I spoke to the driver on the way to the hospital, "Raghav, I have never seen you so irresponsible before. You are working as my driver for almost ten years. Am I right?"

He glimpsed in the rear-mirror to catch a quick sight of my facial expression and nodded before moving his eyes back on the street.

"Just look for some other cook! I can't afford this unnecessary chaos in my life," I ordered, riffing through my schedule of that particular day. He nodded quietly.

After a couple of mute minutes, he said, looking at the rear-mirror, "Sir, she needs your help."

"What do you mean?" I asked, frowning.

"That intruding bastard is Radha's husband, a rickshaw-puller of Paharganj area. He earns nothing and takes all of Radha's hard-earned money for alcohol and gambling. He beats her every day after returning home drunk. Somehow, she is managing to raise her kids, saving tiny amounts every day. Still, she isn't able to send her kids to school," he informed with few pauses as the traffic on the road demanded his attention.

"She has been trying to get rid of him since years. I thought your house would be a haven for her where she can earn and keep herself and her kid away from that animal," he added.

After several minutes of silence when I got down from the car, I told him, "Let her continue."

No, I was not a messiah; neither was I trying to be a vigilante. I did not even know her other than that tiny part of her miserable life. Kindness was an alien feeling to me. But, somewhere deep in my mind, I had decided to make Radha's life a fairy-tale, something she could not even imagine. I wanted to make her the queen of her own life to take all decisions according to her wishes as she had reminded me of my childhood and had gifted me a reason for me to live to my futile life.

That day I had seen her for the first time, vividly under the bright sunshine. She was busy washing a pile of clothes near the tube well. Her complexion had an impeccable ochre hue, glowing, reflecting in the sunlight. She had a boyish physique with toned and lean muscles. One by one, she kept all the washed clothes in a wide plastic tub. It became too heavy for her to carry, so she dragged the tub till the thread where she could hang those clothes to dry. Her wide shoulders gradually tapered to her thin waist. Her mounted breasts huddled together, making a deep cleavage as she was wringing the clothes. She had to stretch out her hand to reach the thread higher than her, revealing her wet navel; deep enough to darken in shadow, surrounded by a popped-up abdominal muscle to form the shape of a clay-lamp. Her wet blouse failed to conceal the absence of her brassiere. The countless bruises and scratches, spread all over her skin manifested the misery of her life. She was like a fallen nymph, exiled from heaven, shackled to satiate the malicious wishes of an aggressive demon who was not satisfied even after tearing off her feathery wings of liberty. He had gone further to proclaim his possession, ploughing his ruthless signatures all over her body.

All of a sudden, she looked straight at me, as if she had been pretending till then to be unaware of my presence and my furtive watch on her from the second floor window. She had brave, wolfish eyebrows over her bluish-green eyes; calm but eloquent, pained but aspirational and capable of reading the core of anyone's mind. The scar on her forehead along with her sharp nose and thin lips was complimenting the beauty of her chiselled face. I moved away from that window embarrassed.

I became addicted to stalking her all the time whenever I was home. Eventually, her discomfort of being watched transformed into anticipation. Many times, I noticed her busy eyes in search of me at all the windows facing the backyard and her effort to stay out of her small outhouse for a longer time. We had begun liking each other's presence. I started returning home for lunch, sometimes in the middle of the day without any reason and often early in the evening. She was not as good a cook as Sanjivani had been. Anyway, it was not her cooking that had been luring me to return home every moment, but that moment when she used to come closest to me to serve food. She had an undiluted, sweet smell what I was addicted to inhaling. It was not the aroma of any artificial perfume; it was the raw smell of her skin.

However, there was an unending distance, an interminable silence and firm ice between us until that night when I saw her stealing ice cubes from the refrigerator. Though I had been noticing the vanishing ice cubes from the fridge in the past, but prior to that night, I had never paid any attention to it. I tailed her to the outhouse while she was carrying the ice cubes in a plastic bag. I had to hide behind a wall nearby hastily as she turned back to close the door immediately after entering the outhouse. I reached that closed door tiptoeing. I waited there for a few moments in hesitation before my morbid curiosity got the better of me and I peeped into the house through that only partly opened window. The only feeble light in the corner of the room made the shadows of different objects lengthier and darker. An infant in a white frock and a teenaged boy were sharing the only furniture of that room, a tiny cot. That ice cube bag was kept by a large metal trunk which was placed adjacent to the wall. To my surprise, she arrived in front of that trunk from some corner of the room while I was wondering about her presence there. She knelt down and pulled out a small mirror, opening the trunk with a loud clang which woke the infant. She got up hurriedly, rushed to that cot, leaving the mirror on the floor and cautiously picked up that infant in her arms. She wrapped that little one in a towel-sized piece of cloth and started swinging her arms in a harmonic motion. Radha was humming and sometimes making typical sounds which signified her inability to talk; a mute angel who could not even express her agony and love.

A smirk popped up on my face spontaneously, feeling pity for those theists who believe in some imaginary supremacy to save them during crisis. Humans would never dare to kill goats or cows in the name of religious sacrifices if they were born with sharp teeth and long claws to scratch out flesh from the human body; it always about the survival of fittest. God does not exist.

After a while, that innocent newborn was deluded effortlessly to consider her mother's lap as the securest place in this world to sleep. Radha placed her on the bed softly before returning to the trunk. She pulled off the saree from her shoulder, letting it fall on the floor quietly and unbuttoned the tight blouse, revealing her firm and mounted breasts. That faint light in the room made those bite marks around her nipples, bruises and fresh wounds all over her breasts vibrant and cast a prolonged shadow up to her abdomen. She held the mirror in her left hand and pressed one ice-cube delicately on one of those wounds. She moaned, sniffing heavily; the light and shadow were playing hide and seek with the oscillating movements of her breasts while breathing. The ice cube started melting, absorbing the heat of her body and dripping on the floor. One by one, she touched all her wounds with ice cubes before sliding her hand inside the petticoat. She lay on the floor, closing her eyes in pleasure. Slowly, the melting ice cubes drenched her petticoat as her hand hustled inside it. She squeaked and a drop of tear rolled down the corner of her eyes. I took my eyes off of that hole and returned home.

"Yes, Samim. What's up?" Ahi asked, accepting the call as her mobile rang, flashing Samim's name on the screen.

"Hey hottie, when are you coming back?" he asked in a modulated British accent.

"I have no idea as of now," she replied inattentively, looking at the manuscript and after a couple of seconds, she added, "But, I have decided one thing. I will publish this manuscript under our imprint, even if I can't get a signature. I just can't let this bestseller remain untold. It's so intense and touches different chords of human psychology; the best piece of writing from Devang Awasthi. And if we are lucky enough to publish it as Awasthi's work, this book will shake the nation."

"But, we might face legal issues," Samim interrupted. "By the way, have you got any breakthrough yet?" he asked with an intention to make Ahi realize the reality.

"I got the typewriter that had been used to write this manuscript and let me answer your next question. Yes, this typewriter types the exact same broken 'T' and 'S'," Ahi argued, trying hard to justify her stay, though somewhere in her mind she was quite certain about her failure to get the signature. In fact, she was arguing with herself.

"And how is that going help you?" he asked, not trying to deceive her this time. He wanted her to come back to Kolkata and spend the Puja with him and her family.

"It will help me to convince that lady that I am not lying," she replied, irritated.

A silence overpowered their conversation.

"I want to tell you something," he said, breaking the silence.

"Yes," she whispered.

Samim sighed and said, "Something special, that I haven't told you before. So, I want to tell you that looking into your eyes, holding your hands and being on my knees. And that is not possible on the phone."

Ahi kept quiet for some time. But, in the next moment, she wondered whether it was a joke to divert that topic and make her smile, as on many occasions he had done the same. However, he was true to his feelings during each of those occasions, but had to manifest them as jokes in the fear of losing her friendship forever.

"Oh! Not again!" Ahi responded, laughing.

It was thirty minutes past five in the evening when Ahi reached Awasthi Nivas. The sun fell behind the bungalow, painting the sky with the last red and orange rays before twilight beckoned the stars. Awasthi Nivas seemed like a dark and colossal pre-historical animal, protecting a nymph from the heat of the sun, casting its never-ending shadow on her.

Ahi planned to visit Hari the next morning, but after realizing the impatience and worries of her sulking mother, she had to take that desperate step. Samim was not happy either. Though that morning's incident was still haunting her as she was out there on the street, she reached Awasthi Nivas, gathering the sprinkled pieces of her confidence and courage as she was determined to publish that manuscript.

She wondered whether Hari had been staying in that same outhouse in the backyard. She reached there, tiptoeing quietly. The lawn at the back was separated by wooden fences from the adjacent house. That abandoned and demolished house at the corner of that lawn bewitched her. She started approaching it like an insect attracted to light.

"Beti, when did you come?" someone asked. Ahi turned back hastily in shock to find Hari. He was standing just behind her.

"Hari uncle, I need your help," Ahi pleaded like an adorable kid. Hari nodded generously.

"Is this Devang Awasthi's typewriter?" she inquired, swiping her mobile screen to show the pictures of that typewriter from different angles.

Hari stared at one of the pictures for a few seconds and then instructed her to navigate the screen back and forth a few times before confirming, "Yes, this is his typewriter."

A wave of enthusiasm blew through her spinal cord inciting her to embrace Hari. But she confined her excitement and just expressed her gratitude.

"Where did you get that?" Hari encountered.

"It was the effect of your lucky tea, sir," Ahi replied with a mischievous smile.

Hari proposed, grinning innocently, "Then let's have another cup of tea. I will make it the luckiest for you this time."

"No uncle, it is late already. I have to go now. Some other day, for sure," she requested.

Hari nodded, rejecting her pleading and started walking towards the entrance of the bungalow. Ahi had to follow him, reluctantly.

"Hari uncle, let me leave. I will come some other day. Otherwise, if that lady arrives in the meanwhile, she will scold you again and insult me also," Ahi requested, explaining her reason.

"You wait inside my home until I bring the tea. Don't worry, she will never come to my house," he comforted Ahi and started walking again.

"By the way, who is that lady?" she asked, following him.

"Devang Sahab's second wife, a real witch," he answered, walking hurriedly towards the bungalow.

"Wait here, I will be back with your tea quickly," Hari stated, pushing open the door of a small house at the opposite side of the bungalow, just by the metal gate at the entrance of the large lawn in front of the bungalow. Ahi had never noticed the check-post like small house at the sideway of the entrance during her first visit to that place.

She stepped inside the house speculatively as Hari departed. It was a just an unpartitioned space, surround by four exposed brick walls and covered with an asbestos ceiling. One corner of it was being used for cooking, Ahi guessed from the utensils gathered there along with a stove on the floor. She settled herself awkwardly on the cot which seemed quite wide for a single person, while that room had no luxury to accommodate that much space. Her eyes fell on a red saree, black blouse and a book kept on the bed behind her as she was exploring that new place out of curiosity. Hari uncle must be staying with his wife, she concluded. However, that book bewildered her completely. She questioned whether his wife was educated enough to read an English book on human psychology. She flipped through a few random pages casually, out of habit, and noticed a few highlighted lines.

"Impressive," Ahi whispered to herself, weighing the seriousness of that book's reader.

All of a sudden, a hollering male voice disrupted that soothing silence around, "Hari… Hari!"

Ahi came out of that house in a hurry, nervous and confused to find a man in jeans, a leather jacket, tall, fair and clean shaven in a funky hat and red shoes. He did not require any introduction as she found a striking resemblance to Devang Awasthi. Must be Dhruv, she guessed.

A huge Range Rover was parked in the middle of that lawn, leaving a trail of mud on the ground that hinted at the speed of that metal giant before the halt. The music inside the SUV was loud enough to suppress the boisterous chorus of the bohemian men drinking inside that vehicle.

"Wow," he beguiled, walking towards Ahi woozily.

"Hari uncle is not here," Ahi informed voluntarily, in an attempt to get rid of him. "You can find him inside the bungalow, most probably in the kitchen," she added desperately as he came too close for comfort. She moved her face away from him to avoid the intolerable odour of alcohol.

"Who the hell are you?" he enquired, slurring, leaning closer to her face. Ahi's earlobes, nasal tip, and cheeks turned red. She stepped back.

"Ahi Chatterjee," she replied, hesitantly.

"Oh! That bong spy," he mocked, smirking. "I am so jealous, that *thulla* (indecent word to address the police) is so lucky to have a sexy bitch like you to work under him. *Garam karti hogi na tu uska?*" he teased, abolishing the gap Ahi had created between them.

She felt her dried out throat as she gulped in panic, looking at the expression on his face. The moist film on Ahi's eyes made her vision blurred. Her face was emitting heat in humiliation as she attempted to step back. She failed, touching her back on the wall. She was desperately looking out for a way to escape. He made a barrier around her, putting his palms on the wall beside her.

In the meanwhile, Hari returned, rushing cautiously to balance the tea tray in his hand.

"Chhote Sahab, please let her go. She is innocent," Hari requested, slavishly.

Dhruv laughed out loudly, clapping like a psychopath and murmured, "Innocent spy!" The dripping lust from his face made Ahi cringe as he was sniffing her neck like a dog.

"I… I have no clue what… what you are talking about. I don't work for the police. I just need a signature from any one of your family to publish your father's manuscript. I am an editor and run a publishing house. You… you can Google," Ahi informed, fumbling with an irregular tempo under a single breath.

"Oh! I have never slept with a bong, intellectual and sexy bitch," Dhruv smutted, caressing her jaw. His menacing act raised her heartbeats. She pushed him back on impulse and tried to run away, but failed, as Dhruv tugged her back violently, gripping her hand firmly. He embraced her in his arms from behind and whispered, "Do you moan in the rhythm of Tagore's song while having sex?" He sang in his faulty pronunciation, "*Akela chalo re…*"

His grip loosened on Ahi as Hari pulled him back forcefully. He slapped Hari, turning back promptly. The other men started stepping out of the SUV.

In that moment, Ahi freed herself from the grasp of Dhruv and started running towards the metal gate. She had to take her sandals off as its heels were sticking on the wet mud of the lawn, beneath the layer of grass. She crossed the lawn, running bare feet and stumbled over the gate as she looked back, wondering whether any of them was chasing her. She stood up with mud all over her jeans and bleeding knees and hands. She pushed open the gate and started running in that dark alley outside the bungalow. She kept running wherever her pair of eyes guided her to. She started breathing through her mouth to grasp more air. One of her sandals slipped from her hands accidentally but she kept running. All of a sudden, she stepped on a stone and started limping. She was scared to death, thinking of Hari, as she knew that those uncivilized, ruthless and spoiled brats would not show any mercy. However, she was helpless to do anything other than pray for him, bursting into tears in anger and helplessness.

She gathered a bit of nerve, hearing the sound of traffic from the main road. However, the tapping sound of boots behind her made her fearful again. She was too terrified to look back and started hopping on her one leg hurriedly in a desperate attempt to reach the end of that gloomy alley. She preferred to believe that the person behind her was just an uninvolved passer-by. However, her belief transmuted into a dilution to her senses after reaching the main road, as the shadow of that person started walking in the same direction as her. She stopped abruptly to confirm the intention of that shadow behind her and the shadow did halt, transforming all her doubts into intense fright.

Several minutes had passed hobbling and beckoning each passing vehicle on the road to get rid of that haunting shadow, but none of them bothered to stop.

All of a sudden, her eyes fell on three policemen, smoking in front of a roadside tea-stall. She rushed to them and started hollering, "Sir, please arrest him. He has molested me and severely beaten an old man."

Those three policemen stood there perplexed for a few seconds before throwing away their half-smoked cigarettes and chorused, "Sir," saluting in unison.

"This is disgusting," Ahi shouted in frustration. "Just because he is rich and well connected, you won't arrest him, right? I will complain against all of you. Because of policemen like you, girls are so insecure and helpless in NCR!" she screamed to attract the attention of the people on the road.

"Madam, please calm down and let me know in details whatever has happened to you," the shadow said in a husky voice behind her.

She turned around to find a tall man in a white linen shirt, neatly tailored to fit his sinewy body and a pair of denims. His sleeves were folded over the elbows, exposing the bulged-out veins on his tanned forearms. The thin and deep gap between the pectoral muscles of his chest and evident collarbone were visible as he kept the first two buttons of his shirt unbuttoned. His muscles were obvious even through his shirt; particularly his wide shoulders, chest, and biceps that stretched out the fabric of his shirt. He had a crew cut just above his lengthy and glossy forehead. He had a pair of thick and perfectly arched eyebrows with a cut mark over his left eyebrow just to make his face imperfect, yet irresistible. His dark brown eyeballs were fixed on Ahi's eyes. His sharp nose and half-dome cheekbones sat above a chiselled jaw, draped with a scruffy beard and moustache around his thin lips.

Ahi had to try hard to preserve her annoyance, concealing the pleasance beneath her frowned face and asked, "Who the hell are you, and why should I say anything to a stalker like you? Do you know who I am?"

"Do you know who I am?" he echoed and smiled, creating a deep dimple on his right cheek. "In NCR, you can't find a single person to answer this question. And surprisingly, most of the people ask me this question in particular."

Ahi managed to freeze her melting rigidness on his dimple, widened jaws, enlightened pair of eyes and enchanting voice.

"Mister whoever you are, I am not in a mood to joke," she rebuked, sustaining her crankiness.

"I am ACP Abhimanyu Rathore," he introduced himself, advancing his hand towards Ahi. She forwarded her hand unconsciously. His handshake was warm, firm and lingering. He twisted her hand softly, to examine the wounds on her elbow and forearms. Ahi savoured his rough and strong touches on her skin. His minty cologne just worked like an ointment for her wounds.

"Dubey ji, please arrange some first aid for madam," he ordered one of those three fellow policemen.

"Yes sir," Dubey ji responded before departing.

"I am absolutely fine. Can we go to Awasthi Nivas, please? I am concerned about Hari uncle; he is too old to tolerate the torture of those ruthless and drunk men," Ahi pleaded.

"Sharma ji, Chaddha ji, let's go! And leave a message for Dubey ji to join us at Awasthi Nivas," Abhimanyu instructed. He jogged to the back of that tea stall and reached Ahi, driving his Royal Enfield.

"Let's go. It's party time," he said, gesturing Ahi to get on his bike with a contented smile.

Ahi expressed a pseudo reluctance, frowning deliberately and sat on the bike, pretending that she had no alternative. They started for Awasthi Nivas, followed by the other two policemen on another bike behind them. The bumpy ride on the potholes of that gloomy alley scared Ahi enough that she had to hold Abhimanyu firmly. She felt his ripped abdominal muscles as she pressed her palm on his stomach firmly. She relished the feeling of giving up her life in the hands of that tough man, holding all the power of manoeuvring that giant machine. The bright and beaming headlight along with the thumping sounds at even intervals of his metallic acolyte wiped out all fear from Ahi's heart.

They entered Awasthi Nivas without any fuss as the entrance was wide open and parked their bikes near the SUV. Ahi rushed to the unconscious old Hari lying on the lawn, bleeding from his face. The tea tray and broken pieces of the teacup were scattered around him. Ahi kneeled down on the spot abruptly and placed his head on her lap cautiously. He was breathing, thankfully.

"*Yeh lo, thulle ki barat a gayi,*" Dhruv shouted, mocking the policemen, including Abhimanyu. "All your tricks to send a spy failed. You are such a dumbass, Abhimanyu, but I should appreciate your choice. Such a sexy bitch she is," he added, giggling loudly. His friends joined him in laughter and clapping, like his obedient dogs in unison.

Abhimanyu pretended as if they did not exist there as he picked up Hari like a feather in his strong arms and ordered, "Sharma ji, call something, whatever you get first on the road," rushing towards the road. Ahi followed him.

An auto-rickshaw arrived in front of the entrance. Sharma ji stepped out of it in a hurry. They managed to lay Hari cautiously onto the backseat of the auto-rickshaw.

"Please get in," Abhimanyu requested Ahi, pointing to the rest of the unoccupied portion of the backseat. Ahi sat there. Sharma ji somehow managed to park his right buttock on the driving seat with the driver. The auto-rickshaw vanished into the darkness, almost in a blink.

Abhimanyu returned to that place where Dhruv and four of his friends were enjoying the shares of marijuana puffs and said calmly, "Mr Dhruv Awasthi, I am arresting you for molesting a woman and violently beating a senior citizen."

All of them burst in laughter as Dhruv disdained him, "*Abe thulle*! Stay within your limits."

Abhimanyu smiled, grabbed Dhruv by his collar and tugged him along towards the road.

"Hey, I am warning you. You will regret your action the most," Dhruv shouted, trying hard to dislodge himself from Abhimanyu's grasp.

His friends hastened towards Abhimanyu, firming their fists. Abhimanyu pulled out his gun which was tucked inside the back of his jeans and aimed it at them. He smiled and warned calmly, "In India, everyone has the right to self-defend themselves. Plus, I am an ACP. I get medals to kill street dogs like you."

All of them firmed their feet on the ground like statues.

"Count my words *thulle*; I will fuck you hard. I will destroy your career and leave you on the street to beg for your own death," Dhruv continued his admonishment, fidgeting aggressively. "Your bosses are just my pet dogs. I will fuck you so hard that you will have to shit through your mouth, asshole."

"Chaddha ji, take him to the police station and lock him up," Abhimanyu ordered, smirking. His face was glowing with satisfaction. He tucked his gun back into the same place, walked down the street and lit a cigarette.

Inspector Chaddha handcuffed Dhruv and took him away.

"Sir, we have admitted Hari. Doctors have taken him to the emergency ward and his treatment is in progress," senior constable

Sharma informed Abhimanyu as soon as he reached Maxima Hospital in sector nineteen.

"That's good. Hope he recovers soon so that we can collect his statement early morning tomorrow," Abhimanyu anticipated, optimistically as his eyes glittered in ambition.

"Dubey ji, how is that lady doing?" Abhimanyu asked, noticing sub-inspector Dubey approaching them.

"She is absolutely fine as her wounds are superficial. The nurse has bandaged her sprained ankle and the lacerations on her hands and leg." He added after a pause, "But, her ankle may stay bruised and swollen for a while and putting weight on that foot can be difficult for her, especially while walking."

Abhimanyu nodded in apprehension, toughening his jaw.

"Is there any point of arresting Dhruv? Anyway, we will have to let him go tomorrow morning. His lawyer will arrive at the police station with a bunch of papers," Sharma asked disappointingly, taking off the cap from his head.

"I am sensing a different story this time. But, we will have to collect the statement of this girl tonight to register an FIR. We don't have the luxury to wait until tomorrow morning," Abhimanyu said in a low voice, as if he was planning something in his mind and then ordered firmly, "Get her statement as soon as her treatment is over. If she can't go to the police station, just record her statement in your mobile here. By any means, the FIR should be perfectly registered by tomorrow evening."

"Yes sir!" sub-inspector Dubey and senior constable Sharma responded in unison.

"And… yes, have two policemen to guard Hari…" Abhimanyu added in brief, moving his fingers around thoughtfully and rushed to Ahi as she came out to the same corridor.

She lurched, balancing her weight on her right leg. She had a walking-stick in her left hand to keep her left feet up in the air and a nurse was guiding her with verbal instructions. She was doing good, but all of a sudden, she attempted to walk normally, putting her left foot on the floor as Abhimanyu reached her.

"How many times should I tell you the same thing … don't put weight on your injured foot! You have to listen to me if you want to be fit quickly," the nurse said.

"You are gorgeous like an angel. Maybe an angel in a bandage but still stunning, adorable and charismatic. It doesn't matter how you walk, you know," Abhimanyu praised after gesturing that nurse to be a little polite.

Dubey ji and Sharma ji exchanged glances, smiling. The gloomy embarrassment that overcast Ahi's face till then evaporated as a pleasant and shy smile lit her face. Her own feelings surprised her like a swimmer in the sea is surprised, detecting her feet will never reach the bottom of the sea and she will be flowing away helplessly. Ahi was carried away in the water of ecstasy. She questioned herself about why she was so happy.

That nurse helped Ahi to sit on a chair near the reception.

"So, I didn't get a chance to know who you are. Let's start from the beginning," Abhimanyu asked.

"I am Ahi Chatterjee, founder of Ankur Publication," she replied, cautiously. The carefree Ahi seemed to be covered under the guise of a shy and speculative newly-married bride.

"So, Ahi, we are expecting your cooperation to register your statement as an FIR against Dhruv. Sharma ji will ask you a few questions, just answer them and please don't try to twist or hide anything," Abhimanyu requested, resting his back on the edge of the reception table.

Ahi nodded like an obedient student. Senior Constable Sharma started enquiring Ahi regarding her occupation, purpose of visiting Awasthi Nivas frequently in the last few days, her permanent address at Noida, etcetera.

A car had been arranged to drop Ahi at Jaideep's flat twelve in the night after all the formalities were completed.

Ahi's mobile rang for the third time and fell silent after a few minutes, failing to make even the slightest crack in her sleep. She was restless and tired at the same time, both physically and psychologically. She was scared to look forward and curious at the same time to get to the bottom and to taste the success of publishing that manuscript.

Her mobile rang again. She grasped the phone, hiding her face on the pillow and glanced at its screen through her partly opened eyes; it was an unsaved number.

"Hello," she responded groggily.

"May I speak to Ahi… Ahi Chatterjee," a modulated voice of a woman who seemed quite familiar to Ahi, asked.

"Speaking," Ahi replied monosyllabically, waiting eagerly for the response.

"Good morning Ahi, this is Maya, Devang's wife. Coming straight to the point without any drama, I have a deal for you."

"What kind of deal?" Ahi asked, shaking off the lazy cloak of the early morning dizziness.

"Withdraw your complaint and I will sign on your agreement to publish that manuscript," she proposed firmly.

"How can you support him? I can understand your feeling as a mother, but you are a woman first, and then a wife and mother. How can you support your son who has molested a woman and beaten an old man so brutally?" Ahi argued, pulling out a cigarette from its packet.

"He is not my son… step… son," she said lengthening the spell of each word as if she wanted Ahi to remember that fact. Ahi was quite shocked by her strange reaction. Why was she so agitated to accept Dhruv as her son, and why was the word 'stepson' so comforting to her?

"Okay… But, how all of a sudden have you started believing that I am not a spy working for Abhimanyu?" Ahi asked, lighting the cigarette.

"I saw the copy of your complaint and your details in it. The FIR is not registered yet, as you haven't signed it. You don't need to visit the court in order to quash the complaint. All you need is to request the investigating police officer to dispel it," she responded promptly as if she had rehearsed those words devotedly and asked after a momentary pause, "If you are done with your questions, can I get your decision?"

"I need some time to think about it. I will call you back," Ahi replied, hung up the phone and took a deep drag from the first cigarette of her day.

Several conflicting opinions, perceptions and arguments were whirling in her mind like the smoke of her cigarette. What should have been prioritised? She could not miscue the opportunity of publishing that manuscript. Not after all that she had been going through just for that manuscript. On the other hand, her importunity to punish that misogynist was not encouraging her to withdraw the allegation. She wondered whether Hari uncle's FIR alone would suffice. She thought of seeking guidance from her father about that legal procedure, but she refrained as they would panic. Was she being selfish? Beyond everything, she was the daughter of the DGP.

Ahi was not convinced enough to buy her dream at the cost of her dignity, or was it just her arrogance and ego that was becoming the obstacle. She picked up the manuscript to fortify her alter ego – greedy and selfish enough to enjoy the triumph at any price and started reading.

Twin flames or twin souls, an unscientific and illogical concept that I would have never believed if I would not have met Radha. According to the concept of twin souls, they are complimenting parts of each other, separated after their birth, and meet each other only in both of their last lifetime on the earth after several incarnations. Each of us has only one twin soul to ascend together after gathering experiences in several past lives and complete the circle of incarnation on this planet. These twin flames could sense the immense attraction as they counter each other for the first time in their lives. This attraction may not be mandatorily physical or spiritual, but it has to be karmic. Their karmic attraction brings them together to share the deepest needs, desires, dreams and darkest portions of their souls.

Yes, I met my twin soul, Radha. That brief stealthy observation of her life through the door-hole was enough for me to know her deeply. Though we had never communicated, and though she was not able to speak, I had listened to her soul and absorbed each drop of her spirit. She was another me, and had been going through similar phases of life. She had the same body as mine, brutally disrupted by her master.

However, I had no clue why her wounds were so fresh as I had not seen her husband after that night. I could not sleep that night as I was thrilled to find her in my life and worried about her relief from all the pains of her life simultaneously.

"How did this happen?" Jaideep enquired shockingly and indicated Ahi's bandaged feet.

"It's nothing uncle, I just fell on the street. I will run after few days," Ahi tried, but failed to convince him.

"Why didn't you tell me? When did it happen?" He darted a couple of questions in disbelief as he knelt down beside Ahi's bed.

Ahi read his face and answered to comfort his senses "Last night… I did not want to bother you so late in the night."

"You are my responsibility till you are in Noida. I am grateful to your father for many reasons in the past and this is the first time he has asked for my help. Please let me do my duty," Jaideep said emotionally, leaving Ahi perplexed for a moment.

"Don't worry, uncle. I would have called you if it was that serious," Ahi said holding his hand. He nodded.

After some mute moments, he said excitedly, "Oh! I totally forgot the main thing; actually, I came to inform you that I have to go to Kolkata for a few days. So, let me know if you need something from there."

"Yes uncle, I don't know how many more days I have to stay here. So, I need some of my clothes. I will tell my mother to keep everything packed. Can you please bring those?" Ahi requested, expecting the obvious answer from him.

"Of course," he assured with his usual grin that comforted Ahi a bit. "Please take good care of yourself in my absence," he added, leaving the room. Ahi smiled back.

"And please don't tell my parents about all this," Ahi pleaded making an adorable face. He turned and smiled before leaving.

Ahi made herself a cup of coffee and started reading again.

Few more days passed by before the secret of her revived injuries was revealed to me. I doubted my eyes as I was drunk enough; that could lead all of my five sensory organs to malfunction. Still, it did not turn out to my illusion that two silhouettes were crossing the lawn in that darkness out there; one of them was limping with the help of two crutches. They passed the bungalow, approaching Radha's house. I lurched down to the ground floor, stumbled several times over the furniture in the drawing room, crossed the corridor, groping the wall cautiously, came out the bungalow and managed to reach in front of her house staggering.

I kept my eyes glued on that door-hole to identify those silhouettes which transformed into two vividly detailed men under the light in the room – her husband and a handicapped man who I had never seen before. He had distorted limbs. One of his legs shrank like a dried-out bottle gourd, hanging in the air from his waist. His skinny hands were awkwardly long up to his knees, joining the tiny palms and inflexible crooked six fingers. He left his pair of crutches casually, resting on the wall nearest to him and moved towards Radha, leaping on his stronger leg. His eyes glittered in immense hunger of lust. Radha moved back a few steps, frowning in disgust.

"Wait…" her husband slurred. "First, get me thousand rupees," he demanded as that handicapped person turned back to him. He handed over some notes to her husband.

"Enjoy…" her husband permitted, cackling while counting the money. Radha hustled into the bathroom and locked the door before they could catch her. Her husband followed her promptly.

"Open the door," he shouted in anger, thumping on that closed door. He waited for a second before banging the door violently, yelling, "Why are you behaving like a virgin, bitch? This is not your first time." She kept the door shut. He kicked the door a couple of times. That teenager boy awoke to the loud noises around him and sat straight by that sleeping infant on the bed in shock. He resembled Radha's husband.

"Come out, you whore… otherwise, I will shout in front of that bungalow till you are kicked out from this house," he admonished abusively.

He tugged Radha hastily as the door opened partly, leaving her to stumble on the floor. She started bleeding from her forehead as her head struck the wall. He picked up the broomstick from the corner of the room and started beating her ruthlessly. Radha begged, making an indistinct cry, holding his feet to buy his kindness. However, he *kept beating her until the broom broke. He threw the stick away and pulled her up grasping her hand and pushed her towards that handicapped person. She stood in the middle like a toy as that person took off her saree, dancing around her on his one leg. He tore her blouse apart, divulging her breasts and jumped on her. She fell back on the floor, failing to bear the thrust of his weight. He rode on her, licking her face, like an ugly chameleon had captured a butterfly with its sticky, long tongue. Her husband claimed his share of her, joining that chameleon in a minute.*

That boy seemed to be mentally challenged to comprehend what was happening around him, as he started clapping insanely.

Their elongated sexual torture turned brutal with slapping, biting, scratching and twisting her body with her moaning in pain.

I returned to my room as I could not tolerate that ruthless ferocity, being just a mute spectator. I poured some whiskey, letting a few ice cubes to float on it. The Macallan Lalique, sixty-two-year-old single malt scotch, blended stealthily and smoothly in blood to unveil my alter ego which was more calm, cruel and intelligent. It always helped me knit my plan flawlessly.

Murder is an art if it can be accomplished untraceably. That night, I might have rescued her, but that could have jeopardized my self-preservation, leaving that ugly chameleon as a witness of my rage on Radha's husband. I do not share my arts with anyone; only I have the proprietorship on them. I don't even believe in that theory of 'an enemy's enemy is my friend'. Hence, I couldn't believe even Radha in this matter.

The basic criterion of a perfect murder is to stalk the prey and keep stalking until the life of that victim has not absorbed in the subconscious mind of the murderer. Gradually, the assassin starts living the life of the quarry. Till then, I had murdered only those people who had shared some portion of their life with mine. But, Radha's husband was lucky enough to have no such business that could facilitate me anytime, space, scope or any excuse to be around him. Being compelled of not having other choices, I had decided to spend a few days of life in the slums of Paharganj, located just west of the New Delhi railway station.

However, before all of those, I had to take care of my twin flame. I was awake the whole night, eagerly waiting for the first sun rays to touch the ground. I vowed to wipe out all the darkness of her life. The last thought of perfection confirmed the plan in my mind while the sunlight fell on me through the window, as if a soft and vulnerable brick of clay had hardened in the fire.

The door was already open as I reached the backyard outbuilding, carrying my medical kit. Radha lay on the floor sideways, huddling her knees to her chest, wrapped with her torn off saree, blouse and petticoat. Bruises, scratches, and blood stains were scattered all over the skin. I gently patted on her cheeks; she did not respond. I was scared to place my finger down to her nostrils as I whispered to myself, "No, you can't give up." I closed my eyes in immense relief when a couple of her gentle exhales touched my finger.

I splashed some water on her face as getting her consciousness back was the first priority for me. She frowned, moaning in irritation.

"Radha, can you hear me?" I asked loudly, slapping her face lightly.

She groaned in pain. Her eyelids quivered as she tried hard to open her eyes, but failed due to the tremendous weakness. Not finding anything other than a kerosene stove in the corner of the room, I went back and got the immersion rod to heat some water in a vessel. But since the power cord was short and couldn't reach the socket while the vessel was placed on the floor, I had to hold the vessel up in the air, wrapping it in a towel, while the water was heating up.

She sat on the floor, huddled, draping herself in that torn saree as I came back to her, carrying the bowl of hot water. She tightened her fist, grasping the saree on her chest as I pulled it gently. She gave an icy stare through her slightly opened pair of eyes, melting its bluish-green colour in lingering tears. I showed her the hot water and a cotton roll to comfort her, affirming my intention. I sat by her for a few minutes, leaving her to be tranquil before my second attempt to unveil her. She loosened her grip slowly and reluctantly as I was removing her saree. I dipped a handful of cotton into that hot water and placed it on a wound on her thigh. She screamed in pain, cowering. I pulled her leg to have a closer look at her wound and found a few scattered glass pieces stuck inside. I pressed my thumbs around that wound as glass pieces cut in both way, either going in or coming out. They had to be taken out. She screamed, gripping my wrist violently.

Slowly, all the glass pieces bugged out of her wound along with lots of blood. She had several similar wounds throughout her body, particularly on her back. It seemed like a ruthless artist had chosen her body as a canvas to craft a masterpiece, lacerating her flesh. I had to spend several hours to clean all her wounds one by one. Eventually, she abandoned her curled up position and lay down on the floor, stretching her limbs. She started moaning lightly in pleasure whenever that soft cotton soaked in warm water touched her wounds. After some time, she fell asleep while I was done dressing all her wounds. I pulled her up into my arms from the floor, lay her on the bed cautiously and *covered her with a bed sheet. Radha's infant girl smiled mesmerizingly, punching her tiny fist in the air. She was pleased to lay by her mother. She had inherited the same bluish green pair of eyes.*

In following few days, I had to take her through several medical tests to detect any injury to her internal organs or any contagious diseases in her blood. These courses taught her to trust a man, perhaps for the first time in her life. I noticed the felicity and the comfort of being secured in her eyes when she used to be around me. She loved to surprise me with her rookie recipes to demonstrate her gratitude. However, that was not quite adequate for me as I wished to see her like a free bird, soaring high in her own terms.

Ahi's phone rang, indicating a message from Maya. It read: *Should I consider your delay as a rejection of my proposal?*

"Wait, lady, wait! Let your stepson feel the fucking heat for sometime," Ahi whispered, simpering and started reading the manuscript again.

Paharganj, the authentic example of the crowded, messy, dingy and noisy backyard of India. The main attraction of this area is innumerable unhygienic and cheap hotels around the main market that joins two railway stations, Ramakrishna Ashram Metro and New Delhi Railway Station. The street of that main market branches out in several alleys that are so narrow that even a cycle-rickshaw can clog them. People from different parts of India and the world flock here every day. Some of them find this place cheap enough to accommodate their tight budget while travelling, while some arrive to nip the cheap pleasure of drugs or to romp with foreign skin through the oldest business of the world, prostitution. Those glitzy alleys which glitter in neon lights are the sloppy and slippery paths that lead headlong to bottomless perdition, luring people to sex and drugs, the ancient origin of all pleasures. And obviously, few people like me take shelter there to hide their identity after or before committing any crime.

I managed to get an accommodation in one of those cheap lodges without exposing my identity as the man at the reception only cared about money from me. They allocated a concrete cell, built with four identical walls, covered in patches and pervert sketches. The only small window of it just above the bedbug-ridden bunk was draped with thick and overlapping spider-nets which merely allowed some lights to enter the room. The wall opposite that window opened to the smallest and dirtiest toilet, I had seen in my entire life.

It reminded me of those fancy-dress competitions at my school as I dressed in the oversized, dirty white pyjama and kurta, along with a piece of plaid to cover my face casually and moderately. I was the weakest contestant of those competitions amongst my classmates. They used to mask their faces under the layer of thick makeup that complemented their appropriate attires to mould themselves in their desired characters of disguise. Most of their parents used to visit the school on those special days to guide their kids to be the best. On the contradictory, my attire used to be the school uniform like any normal day. Though my uniform never won me any award in those fancy-dress competitions, it was my camouflage in reality as I was the survivor in disguise of a student.

New Delhi railway station, sandwiched between Ajmeri Gate and Paharganj is the busiest railway station in India. The sixteen platforms of this world's largest route interlocking system often fall short to accommodate more than four hundred trains and five lakh passengers every day. It was quite difficult to pinpoint him in that ocean of crowds as I reached the cycle-rickshaw stand outside the railway station at nine in the morning. It seemed that many trains had arrived at the same time to ignite an explosion of crowds that overflowed on the street outside the station. It steered all the porters, rikshaw-pullers, beggars and the drivers of all other vehicles towards a competition to secure their morning wages. Eventually, that centralised crowd scattered in all possible direction, as if some mischievous kid had stoned a beehive.

Finally, I could see Radha's husband, lazily lounging on his rickshaw, aloof of all hustle and bustle around him like a saint who had achieved his inner peace, dominating all seven cardinal sins of a human being. He was engrossed in relishing the smoke of his bidi. I glued my eyes on him for the next fifteen days, transforming myself into his shadow. Fortunately, he never met Radha in those days to make me impatient and intolerant. His devil-may-care life was quite limited to few repetitive activities like dozing on his rickshaw or on the street under the influence of some cheap intoxicants, fighting or quarrelling with any random person around him and visiting the brothel. He had a fixed hotel, named Haridwar, in one of those narrow alleys for daily lunch and occasional dinner. There was nothing unusual for me in his life other than that teenaged waiter boy who used to serve him food every day. That boy was a little different due to his effeminate behaviour. He used to pay some money to Radha's husband after serving lunch and had got beaten few times when the amount was less than usual.

However, none of those was part of my business. I was looking for that precise minute in his daily life when he would be alone and could not scream for help, feeble enough to resist me for his breath, longest enough to offer me ample time to accomplish my art, and untraceable enough to keep it secret forever. And I had found my favourite moments when he used to return home in the middle of the night from the brothel or any cheap liquor shop through those dark and empty alleys, staggering and stumbling over his own feet.

The message tone disrupted Ahi's attention. She unlocked the screen to find the message from Maya which read: *Meet me at 10 a.m. outside La Fitness, Sab Mall, roof top, Sector 27, Opposite Maxima Hospital. And don't forget to bring your agreement.*

"Desperate with attitude – a unique piece," Ahi whispered, smirking.

Ahi hustled her pair of thumbs on the mobile's keypad and typed: *Water doesn't come to you when you are thirsty.* But on second thought, she deleted that text. She was convinced to buy the opportunity, costing her pride or ego or whatever that sentiment was that was making her stubborn.

She stepped out of the bed, freshened up, changed her clothes and started for La Fitness in sector 27. Wasting no time, Maya signed that agreement and thanked Ahi.

"Maya ma'am, I should advise you not to be so happy as Hari uncle's complaint must have been registered by now and Dhruv will stay behind bars," Ahi informed, securing the signed agreement in her bag and started walking towards the elevator.

"Miss Ahi, I don't like to be indebted. So, take one advice from me in exchange," Maya said, mopping her forehead with her wristband. Ahi turned back to her, pressing the switch of the elevator.

"Don't involve yourself in this unnecessary mess. I believe your purpose has been served with my signature. So, go back to your city and enjoy your success. I know how to take care of myself and Dhruv," Maya said with a pleasing smile.

Ahi entered the elevator as it reached that floor and the door opened. Maya waved her goodbye as the door was closing, wearing a smile that only disturbed Ahi.

A hi could not help grinning as she was on the way to Indira Gandhi International Airport. Her twinkling eyes and stretched pair of cheekbones under them, tiny and glittering row of teeth peeping through her rosy pair of lips, and occasional brushing of her untied hair on her face due to the breeze through the open car-window was testimony of her internal contentment. She rested her head on the car window to feel the cool breeze of the evening on her face. It was a pivotal evening for her, as finally, she had bagged the permission to publish the novel for her infant publishing house. Everything was like a dream to Ahi. She smiled as her mind ran through her dreams on bare feet like a kid, thinking of her dialogues and others' reactions when she would be describing her success story to her colleagues. She giggled, planning to blend some extra thrill with the truth to make her story spicier.

All of a sudden, she noticed the eyes of her cab-driver on the rear-view mirror. He was thoroughly enjoying her mime to get rid of the boredom of driving in heavy traffic. Ahi became stern, toughening and pretending to be busy with her mobile in embarrassment.

"Fuck you!" she whispered in irritation.

It was Ahi's habit to click on the Facebook icon whenever she unlocked her mobile-screen. She thought of updating a status regarding her breakthrough, but she refrained as she wanted to trick the biggest prankster of her life Samim and surprise her parents. She smiled again and gently bit her lower lips, realising the presence of that cab-driver.

"Madam ji, have you done anything?" the driver asked, making eye contact through the rear-view mirror.

Ahi took some mute moments to get out of the initial shock before replying, "Please concentrate on your driving."

The driver put on the left indicator, slowly drifting the car from the middle of the road towards the left.

"What the hell? What are you doing?" Ahi almost screamed in latent hostility.

The driver halted the car on the shoulder of the street and pulled the hand break violently, avoiding all her questions. Her heart skipped few thumps as a chill passed through her spine. She paled in fright as that part of the road was quite empty, except for the speeding vehicles that were passing them unnoticed. The driver got out of the car, jogged around it to reach the left back door and opened it. Ahi dragged herself to reach the farthest corner on the backseat from that opened door.

"Sorry ma'am, but it will be better for you to surrender," the driver advised, leaning on that door. "It's not possible for anyone to escape from him," he added, sighing, as if Ahi had reminded him of some depressing experiences.

"I think I misjudged you yesterday night, but now I know you very well." A known, husky male voice stated from the car window she had rested her back on. She looked startled, turning back hastily to find Abhimanyu. Ahi sighed in relief. He was looking like a knight in shining armour in his neatly ironed police uniform. The uniform was like his second skin and made only to complement him.

"You know what, you are one of those educated cowards who indulge in blame-game for any mishap in their lives or in our country. Those escapists can only point at others, their parents, teachers, government, police, political leaders, and this whole system," he hollered as Ahi came out of the car, perplexed.

"For people like you, anything is just a Facebook status – a few likes, shares, and debates and then wait for the next incident to be discussed on social networks. But when time comes to act on it in the real world, all you just care about is your career and prosperity," he continued as she stood there, her head hung low. The driver was pretending to be indifferent, looking at the other side of the road.

"I won't force you to do anything, but remember this incident before you blame the police department of NCR next time. You don't deserve to be our judge and always remember we are not aliens. Policemen are the part of your society and your system to follow certain rules, regulations, and procedures," he hissed in one breath.

"I... I am sorry!" Ahi fumbled, playing with the diamond-ring on her finger.

"Do you have any idea how expensive your sorry could be? I had been waiting for the slightest chance to arrest him and my intention had all my attention. I had been keeping track of each and every person around that Awasthi Nivas, hiding in those dark alleys," he informed, concealing his seething anger, frequently toughening his jaws.

"Do you have any personal grudge?" Ahi asked in a low voice.

"No, Miss. Princess of the virtual world. He is a bloody murderer; he killed his father," he whispered, leaning his face close to her face. Ahi savoured that minty smell in his mouth as she closed her eyes in fear, breathing deeply.

"What? Wasn't that a suicide? It was out there on national television and all the leading newspapers," Ahi asked in shock.

"Yes, his family members had stated that to the media to escape from the law. But, I couldn't buy their story as the circumstantial evidences at the scene of the crime pointed to a different story," he said, plunging into deep thought. "We are not appointed to believe only what we see. A crime scene is a murderer's painting where we can see only those things that a murderer wants to show us. We are trained to comprehend the future, sniffing the past and that's what we are paid for," he continued.

"Then, why didn't you arrest ..." Before Ahi could finish her question, Abhimanyu gestured her to be silent, attending an incoming call on his mobile.

"Yes, Sharma ji... what? Where?... I am coming... keep the crime scene untouched," he responded calmly, sandwiching his words in silent moments and rushed towards his bike.

"Someone has murdered Hari in that hospital," Abhimanyu informed as he started his bike parked right behind the cab and vanished on that highway in seconds, leaving Ahi shell shocked.

"Bhaiya, please drop me to Maxima Hospital," Ahi instructed, gathering all her senses back after a few minutes.

"Is everything okay, Madam? I will suggest you follow his orders. He is a dangerous man," the driver advised in a sympathetic voice.

"Could you please mind your own business and drop me there," Ahi requested in a low voice, blending her frustration and despair.

Ahi found it difficult to reach the entrance, pushing through the crowd of localities and media gathered in front of the hospital.

"You can't go any further," ordered one of the five policemen who were trying hard to refrain the crowd to enter the hospital, making a human chain.

"Sir, please allow me. I have to go inside. I know him personally," Ahi pleaded the police-officer.

"So what? Many of these people might know him. I just can't allow anyone inside now," he snapped back in irritation.

Ahi's sight brushed over a known face in the crowd as she glanced the crowd, searching for Abhimanyu. Was it the leader of that transgender group who had rescued her? She scrutinized the crowd, but she was nowhere in sight.

In the meanwhile, Senior Constable Sharma waved that policeman to allow Ahi inside, noticing her in the crowd.

"Third room at the right on the second floor," Sharma informed briefly as Ahi reached him near the reception.

Ahi's feet shook as she started climbing the stairs. She blamed herself for his death. She was ashamed of her selfishness. That old man stood against those besotted hostile group of men in spite of knowing his limitations and she allowed him to get away with it for her fame and career. He gave up his life for her dignity and she sold that for her prosperity. Her eyes were moist, the earlobes and cheeks turned red in ignominy. She wasn't worthy to be called the daughter of DGP Dhritiman Chatterjee.

Abhimanyu exchanged a glance with her, talking to a forensic expert as she entered the room. She glimpsed at Hari's lifeless body on the bed, surrounded by few men in khaki and few in formals. She was reluctant to move closer and waited for those men to move away. She gazed at the cadaver for a few moments perplexedly as few of those officers left the room. The body lay on the bed with the throat savagely slit. The smell of the blood in the room made her sick. She burst out crying, attracting everyone's attention in that room.

Abhimanyu came near her, taking off his gloves and walked her out of the room, embracing her in his arms.

"Control Ahi, control yourself," he whispered, patting on her head as she cried inconsolably, resting her head on his chest. He walked her to the chairs in the corridor. "Sit," he said softly. He made her sit down upon one of those chairs.

"Could you please get her some water," he requested the nurse assigned to help the police in their investigation. She nodded with a smile and left.

"You shouldn't have come here," he said, occupying the chair next to her. "I too shouldn't have allowed you in that room; my bad," he added after a pause.

In the meanwhile, that nurse returned, carrying a glass of water. Ahi drank the water in a single breath, panting after emptying the glass.

"You can still catch your flight if you want. Do you want me to drop you at the airport?" he asked, checking the time on his wristwatch.

Ahi gazed at him in wonder, frowning. "Nope, I was not stalking you," he said, shrugging and pouting to make an innocent gesture. "Actually, I came to know a middle-aged man, Jaideep. He introduced himself as your uncle when I went to meet you," he added.

"I will stay here," she replied in a low voice.

"No, let's go. I will drop you to your place," he said standing up from the chair.

"I will stay in this hospital," she replied stubbornly, gluing her eyes on the wall, opposite to her.

"That's against our protocol, Ahi. Moreover, you are not comfortable in…" he attempted to convince her but before he could finish his words, she screamed insanely, "I killed that man, arrest me."

He placed his palm on her mouth firmly and walked her out of the hospital premises. He tugged her through that over-enthusiastic crowd gathered outside the building, leading her to reach a point a little far from that crowd and chaos.

"Have you lost it completely?" he shrieked, tapping on her head. "Do you have any idea that your statement can be considered as your confession to arrest you for this murder?" he continued as Ahi cried, covering her face with her palms.

He shook her, grasping her shoulders, "Ahi, look at me."

She looked at him tearfully. "You are not responsible for his death. It was my responsibility to protect him and I failed in my duty," he said, toughening his jaws and gazing at her eyes.

"I don't know what to do. I am not able to forgive myself. Guilt is eating me from inside. I never felt so helpless in my life."

"Take that guilt out of your mind," he consoled, sandwiching her palm firmly in his palms. "Even if you would have registered your FIR, it had to happen, as they would have been more desperate in that case," he clarified rationally.

"Can I do something now to get justice for Hari uncle? Maybe that will help me to get rid of this guilt a bit," she asked sobbing.

"I don't believe you anymore, Ahi," he replied, taking his eyes off her face. "I really can't believe a person who goes back on a promises for self-interest," he added, sighing.

She glanced at him in wonder that how he knew about her deal with Maya. He read her face, gloomy in remorse and informed, "Maya called to tease me."

"Sorry! It won't happen again. Please give me a chance," she pleaded.

"Sorry does not change reality, it never did. You won't understand the pain of a policeman. You will never understand our struggle to do justice," he said disappointingly. The soreness on his face was evident to Ahi.

"I do… I do understand a policeman," she whispered. "I have grown up, witnessing the frustration, helplessness, joy and success of a policeman intimately," she continued. He looked at her face; he had a questioning expression.

"I am the daughter of the Director General of Kolkata Police, Dhritiman Chatterjee." She had an expression of pride and shame, together.

"Are you serious, or is it just a stunt to impress me?" he asked in disbelief.

Ahi pulled out her mobile, opened one of her pictures with her father, held the screen in front of his eyes and said, "See!"

"Girl, I am his biggest fan; he is my idol, the guru. I studied all his cases, his interviews, and articles," he said breathlessly. Ahi smiled, seeing his enthusiasm. "He handles his cases with extreme expertise, keeping all the laws intact. I have never seen him give up due to the pressure from the influential people of our society." He took a breathing pause and added, "Moreover, I have noticed that he always relishes cases where the accused is from an influential background."

"Tell me about it! My mother always complains about that," she said smiling.

They kept talking for hours on the way back to Jaideep's flat. The despair and melancholic apprehension of their discussion had lingeringly evaporated as Ahi answered those childish questions of Abhimanyu about her dad.

"I know Bengalis are very fond of fish. So, is it fish that keeps him energetic, sharp and sorted? Or does he do yoga and all?" he asked like a confused kid. Ahi started giggling.

"No, I don't like fish and I... I only go to the gym. So...," he mumbled, fumbling in embarrassment, looking all around. Ahi burst out laughing.

12

Ahi had been waiting for Abhimanyu's call since early morning when she woke up as he had promised to call her to discuss her roles in his investigation. She was feeling quite drained out after the disrupted sleep through that night due to that haunting vision of Hari's dead body. That was the first time she had seen the dead body of a person she had known and who had been killed so brutally.

Several times, she thought of calling him while freshening up and preparing her breakfast. However, she refrained, afraid she'd seem like a desperate dame. Being compelled of the situation, she started reading the manuscript further.

The plinth of a perfect murder mostly depends on the strategy that breeds secretly in the core of a murderer's mind. Gradually, it matures, depleting information, practical facts, minute detailing of the victim, location, time and different scenarios. Finally, the strategy grows wings to accomplish its intention, flying over the reality, while the killer starts precisely selecting convenient instruments and objects. However, the secrecy of these phases plays the most important role for success. Even the tiniest leakage of strategy, because of asking the most trusted person or searching Google for detailed information can jeopardise the perfect murder. I was the seamless from that perspective.

In those days of stalking, I had been visiting my workplace every day in my car, letting my driver witness my journey. I intended to assure my presence to my doctors and employees, meeting as many of them as possible before leaving the hospital in public transport at a different time each day. I had never spent my whole day at Paharganj as I used to stalk a portion of his day at a time and return to the hospital. Though night was my favourite time, I had stalked him in the day as well, as per my rules of stalking. And most importantly, I used to leave my mobile either at home or in the hospital.

Everything had sailed smoothly without any suspicion of the people around me to anchor my confidence on judgment day. I did not forget to perform my ritual of engulfing myself in that white wall of my punishment room. I could see Master in that wall after his death, shackled, scrawny, whipped and bloodied; it always strengthened the devil inside me.

I could have murdered Radha's husband effortlessly, poisoning his drink in those cheap and overcrowded liquor shops, under no surveillance. But, I wanted it to be messy, brutal and painful as he did not deserve an easy escape.

I waited in that benighted alley, camouflaged in a black poncho-raincoat, monkey cap, and gloves after parking Master's old ambassador car by the main road. Master had bought that navy-blue four-wheeler when he started his practice as a doctor, early in his career. I had to fake its number plate to deceive any CCTV camera *over there. I was equipped with a sharp blade integrated straight razor, a coil of nylon rope, a dental elevator, a mandibular extraction forceps, a folded, large polythene sheet, a roll of duct tape, few rolls of cotton and a piece of cloth.*

After a few minutes, I heard the humming of that same, famous and old Hindi song which often I had been humming since I had started stalking him. He crossed me limping and stopped in front of his hut. He fumbled to drop the key on the ground as he attempted to open the door. Few dogs started barking at him. He groped for his key in the darkness of that alley, bending on his knees. He picked up the key along with a few stones from the ground.

"Saale kuttey!" he hollered as he stoned the dogs away.

I tiptoed towards him while he finally opened the door and stood close behind him. I pushed him aggressively as he turned back to close the door after entering the hut. He fell on the floor on his back.

"Abey, tu kaun hai?" he screamed in terror.

I had to be quick, and I believe, I did that as hastily as possible for me. I shut the door from inside, jumped on him to stick the duct tape on his mouth, clamping his hands under my knees. He put up a decrepit protest to resist as I bent his hand at his back, moaning and panting. I hogtied him quite effortlessly with my nylon rope. His bulged-out pair of eyes were gazing at me in disbelief as I arranged that polythene sheet on the floor. He glowered at me, groaning to release his limbs in anxiety as he lay there on his chest. I believe that exercise must have evaporated his intoxication. I rolled him on the floor to place his body in the middle of that polythene sheet. I glimpsed over the entire alley, opening the door just to be sure we were not being watched; everything was according to the plan. I shut the door and returned to him.

He was trying to say something, noising weirdly though his confined lips, but I was least interested in hearing him. I took out the razor and held that in front of his eyes as I wanted to relish the terror of pain and death in his eyes. He started fidgeting. The overflowed tears from his eyes pacified my burning thirst a little. I kneeled down by his face, tugged at his hair to place his head on my thighs and rammed the razor into his head recklessly. It cut the hair along with the scalp and the flesh of his head. He jiggled his head to escape from that blade, but rather it punctured his head severely as blood made a puddle on that sheet. I collected all his hair in a bag and kept that aside.

I flipped him aside and tore off a portion of his shirt to wipe off the blood from his face and head as it was skidding from my grip. It was essential for me to hold his head firmly in order to pull out his teeth; moreover, he was jerking his head constantly. I slit a portion of the duct tape on his mouth to get at his teeth, stuffed that piece of shirt in his mouth and wrapped his stuffed mouth with more duct tape, keeping it open apart. He was groaning feebly. I placed my left knee above his right ear, pushing my entire body weight to firm his head on the ground, letting my two unrestricted hands grip the dental elevator and mandibular extraction forceps. His decayed gums hardly clenched his teeth due to cavities and other infection. A little push of the elevator on the gum accompanied with a sharp tug of the extraction forceps was sufficient to extract them. It took quite an elongated process than my expectation to collect all his teeth in that same bag. I had to allow some time to refrain him from fainting in agony as I wanted him to feel every bit of that pain.

I had already spent quite a long time in preparing the prey for those cute, little and gluttonous creatures, as they are poor to munch human *hairs and teeth. They needed a minimum of six hours to accomplish the best possible finishing touch to my art. I quickly wrapped his nose, ears, and mouth in the duct tape and left him to die. He thrashed about in his own blood on the poly-sheet for few minutes like a fish out of water. His eyes bulged out of his skull as he gradually became tranquil. I noticed a painless internal peace on his face as I untied him.*

The day we arrive in this world, our journey starts towards our death. We are born just to meet our demise; the inevitable, painless, uncomplicated, quiet and aeonian destiny.

I coiled all the ropes and duct tapes and shoved all them together inside that bag where I had kept his hair and teeth. Then, I took off all his clothes, crumpled them together and mopped the blood on the sheet to ensure not a single drop of blood leaked on the floor while wrapping him in the polythene sheet. The bag grew heavier after I put in his blood-soaked clothes, but obviously lighter than his corpse, wrapped in that polythene sheet; a burden for me, Radha and many others like us.

I swayed back to my car, carrying the dead body on my right shoulder and holding the bag in my left hand. I heard some voices as I reached the threshold where the dark, blind alley was joining the comparatively lightened up main road. I had to step back in the darkness, letting them pass by that area. They hung out there for a minute to light their cigarettes; the smokes from them smelled like a fine blend of nicotine and marijuana. I rushed to my car, opened the dickey and laid the dead body cautiously as soon they departed that place. The interior of the trunk was neatly laminated in thick plastic sheet. I was relaxed while driving to meet my partners in crime at Chirag.

A killer and his or her victim are linked through two prime aspects: motive and evidence. My motive to kill Radha's husband was quite lame and irrational for any second person on the earth other than me. The richest doctor of the city and one of the famous authors of the country could not kill the husband of his maid. What could be the motive? Lust, love, revenge and kindness were not the buyable options for the society, as getting a female in my life was not a tough deal for me. Motive can only guide suspicion in the right direction, whereas evidence can get a murderer caught. What if a killer just vanishes? The chief evidence, the corpse of the victim, all other allied evidence like the murder weapon and blood, skin, hair or any other object which can uniquely identify the killer become obtuse due to the absence of the dead body. The dead body is kind of a key to open all the locked doors of a killer's mind where all the secrets are secured.

I supposed to take fifteen minutes to reach my destination at Chirag. However, it took almost thirty minutes as I had to take a detour to skip the police check-post on the way. I had visited that place before several times to be acquainted with the minute details. I parked my car in a dusky place, away from the main gate where the light of the street lamps cast a large shadow. I knocked on that wooden gate, beneath the metal sheet and waited to jump over the last hurdle, holding a piece of cloth soaked in chloroform.

"Abhi bandh ho gaya hai, kaal ana ," my last obstacle responded from inside.

I thumped on the gate a little louder to irritate that guard. He did open the gate after a couple of clangs of metal hinges. Before he could comprehend anything, I pressed that cloth on his nose and mouth. He was shocked and grasped my throat with his left hand as his right hand was insanely groping all over my hands and body in a desperate attempt to get rid of that cloth on his face. I tightened my grip as he scuffled for a few more seconds before collapsing on the ground, tweaking a tiny part of the skin from my hand. Naturally, that skin could have identified, me but do we care about skin cells stuck inside the nail of a living human?

I rushed back to my car, opened the trunk, positioned the cadaver on my shoulder and returned to that place. I staggered to reach that place where those devils were waiting for me, huddling together, surrounded by the wooden fence. I dropped the dead body inside the pigpen, unwrapping the polythene sheet. More than fifty hogs slowly approached the cadaver and surrounded it.

We couldn't have relished bacon on our plates if we were aware that the teeth of a swine can cut through human bones like a knife into butter; flesh and other organs can be gulped without even chewing. It is a jest of nature, creating a swine genetically similar to a human; the blood, flesh and organs, except the brain, are exactly the same. If a human consumes an undercooked pig, that person may ingest crazy parasites that live in our own flesh and brain as well. Even their hearts can replace ours to pump our blood. Their skin can be grafted onto our body to grow there and their blood will keep us alive if it is transfused into our blood. Is it not hilarious?

I returned home and waited for nature's declaration of that night's end, hoping the sunrise would erase all the incidents of last night naturally from the earth.

"Good morning supercop," Ahi greeted, receiving the call.

However, her telepathy failed her as her mother responded in shock, "Supercop? Who is that?" Ahi glanced at the mobile screen, shamefacedly biting the tip of her tongue.

"Nothing Maa, just a friend," she replied, playing her fingers on the manuscript.

"I didn't know that you have any friend who is in the police."

"Uff! Maa, I just tease him like that. Leave it now," she responded, irritatingly. "How are you?"

"As usual, my days are filled with tension for my daughter and my super-cop husband," Ahi's mother said, sighing. Ahi smiled.

"That's your favourite way to kill time. There is nothing to worry," Ahi teased her mother, controlling her smile.

"Huh! Don't talk rubbish," she snapped back, making Ahi chuckle.

"Okay, I will call you later. I am reading now," Ahi said.

"When will you come back? Durga Puja will start in another three days. What will you do there alone during Puja?" her mother grumbled.

"Maa, I have my whole life left to enjoy Durga Puja, being in Kolkata. It's fine… absolutely fine to miss one year. Now don't be so dramatic," Ahi retorted.

"You and your father never listen to me… never. Do whatever you want," her mother screamed before hanging up.

She kept the phone aside and started reading the manuscript again.

I burnt his clothes, hair, all those polythene sheets, and duct tapes along with my clothes, but his teeth. Teeth are the most durable structures that resist destruction more than skeletal tissues. Even the concentrated blend of hydrochloric acid and nitric acid took more than eight hours to dissolve them completely. I flushed that liquid into my commode thereafter.

The murder weapons had turned into innocent medical instruments after a thorough wash. Obviously, the blood stains that are invisible to the naked eye are quite traceable after applying luminol, as this chemical reacts with the iron in the haemoglobin to be noticeable under UV rays. But it was impossible for any human to handpick the murder weapons from a pile of innumerable similar instruments in my hospital.

Last but not the least, Master's ambassador. Its navy blue colour was capable of deluding any video surveillance as all the dark colours guise as black in the darkness and that fake, plastic number plate was not tough to burn.

I started buying almost all the newspapers, especially the local ones to measure the consequences of my deeds of that night. It seemed nobody was bothered about that pig that had been eaten up by the other pigs.

I had visited that piggery farm many times after that night to plan precautionary steps based on the situation. However, other than that bewildered security guard of that piggery farm, nobody was concerned enough to report anything to the police as they had not found any loss or damage to their farm. His story of that night became a source of jest for his colleagues.

There must be human blood mixed in the mud of that pigpen. However, it was not different in colour from the blood of chicken and other meat they had piled in the same pigpen next morning to feed those hogs.

Ahi brooded in a weird sense; the words she had been reading were not fictitious. The real world, its entities, and incidents are much stranger than fiction. She kept the manuscript aside, took off her reading glasses, laid down on the bed and closed her eyes, hoping for a rejuvenating emptiness in her mind.

Ahi woke up to the ring of her mobile phone. The sleep deprivation of the previous night made her sound asleep in the daylight.

"Hello," she responded in a sleepy voice and closed eyes, receiving the call. The mobile screen showed five o'clock in the evening.

"Are you fine? Your voice is not sounding normal." She recognized Abhimanyu's masculine voice.

"Yeah, I am fine; just dozed off, waiting for James Bond since morning," she mocked, yawning.

"Oops! I am sorry," he apologised, laughing. "Actually, we are continuously working since last evening. We have spent almost last eighteen hours on different roads of Noida, Delhi, Ghaziabad, Faridabad and Gurgaon. But after returning home, you're the first one I am calling," he added.

"Oh! Then you should rest now. We will meet tomorrow as per your convenience," she suggested.

"No, I can function without sleep, don't worry. Especially, when I am able to break a tough nut after a hard and long chase." His voice conveyed a seething enthusiasm that defeated his physical weariness.

A vibrant smile lit Ahi's face as she asked, "So, where are we meeting and when?"

"See you at GIP at sector thirty-eight. We can hang out at some coffee shop or some restaurant. Is that fine with you?" he said after a thoughtful mute moment.

"Yup."

"No, I mean if you have any other choice of place, we can meet there as well. I don't know too many places," he said. He smirked and added, "I am habituated to spending most of my time on the road, so I know only a few roadside dhabas."

"I have no problem. And I don't know much about Noida. I don't think my suggestion will be better than your choice either," she replied, smiling. "See you there in thirty minutes."

Ahi quickly freshened up and wore her favourite casual attire – torn jeans, white spaghetti top and an unbuttoned check shirt on top of it. After spraying some perfume and applying lip-gloss, she put her cigarette packet, lighter and money in her wallet before leaving for sector thirty-eight.

Abhimanyu waved as Ahi got down from the auto-rickshaw at the entrance of the Great India Place Mall. She walked down to him slowly, to not hurt her ankle any more. A naughty smile played on her lips, noticing his effort in dressing up like an elegant, sophisticated man in that sky blue, skinny blazer on a white linen shirt that was tucked inside black tapered trousers. The sleeves of his blazer were pulled up, tightly gripping the widening portion of his forearms after the elbows, leaving that large, metal watch to proclaim its existence on his wrist.

"Whoops! Did I spoil your evening?" she asked in pseudo concerned voice, savouring his minty cologne fragrance on the way towards the building of the mall.

"Not at all! Why do you think so?" he enquired.

"Seeing you dressed like that, I thought you are on a date," she replied looking straight into his eyes. They smiled in unison and took their eyes away from each other to hide their blushes. "I would have worn something better, in that case," she added, concealing her smile.

They were silent while they approached the security check at the entrance of the building. However, the lingering smiles on their faces were still talking to each other.

"Your beauty is not dependent on any dress. The dresses should be honoured if you chose them for yourself," he said controlling his heartbeats which were racing furiously under his rib cage. Ahi started giggling on his naïve attempt, leaving him embarrassedly mute.

They reached TGI Friday's on the third floor. An attendant kept the two menu cards on their table after they settled in their chairs and asked, "Ma'am, would you like to have normal water or mineral water?"

"Mineral," Ahi replied promptly, leafing through the menu before Abhimanyu could even understand his question.

"A Jack Daniel's Norwegian Salmon and an Irish coffee," she ordered as the waiter returned with a bottle of water.

"And for you, sir?" he turned to Abhimanyu and asked.

"Same, Sal... Salmon fish and coffee," he fumbled, ordering.

"Abhi, that's not coffee," Ahi whispered, leaning on the table. Then she turned to the waiter, "Could you please allow us some more time to decide?" The attendant nodded and departed.

"Abhi, it's an Irish whiskey; see this," Ahi said, pointing the Irish coffee on the menu.

"I told you, I am clueless," he said, laughing embarrassedly.

Ahi smiled, kept her soft little palm on his tough, large one and said, "Don't worry, I will teach you."

They exchanged smiles. Abhimanyu ordered some chicken wings and soft drink as he had to drive back home.

"Oh! I forgot to tell you the good news and the bad one. We have arrested the killer after a long chase throughout the NCR. The CCTV camera of the hospital made our life a bit easier," he said with a sparkle of pride in his eyes. "But, he is just a junky, had no connection or motive to kill Hari other than earning some money for his addiction. And the bad part is, I had to let Dhruv go," he added.

"That's a relief. But did he say who hired him?" she asked, taking a sip of water.

"Not yet, but I am sure he will speak in front of Dubey ji, Sharma ji or Chaddha ji. This trio is a deadly combination to crack the core of a criminal, both physically and psychologically. They play separate roles to earn the fear, faith, and hope of the criminal and fine tune on the intensity of these three aspects depending on the characteristic of a particular criminal." Abhimanyu relished talking about his work and team, as Ahi's attentive presence encouraged him.

He continued, "I am confident that I will arrest Dhruv again soon based on the statement of this junky. I am just counting the hours now."

"Do you mean that I don't need to contribute anything?" Ahi asked, disheartened. He nodded. "Okay, then I suppose

I should go back to Kolkata," she added, expecting his dissent.

"Can't you stay for a few more days?" he asked, taking his eyes away from her. She gazed at him, expecting his true acquiescence of his heart without any nonsense excuse. "I… I might need your help… you know… may be later sometime," he fumbled. Ahi smiled as she looked away.

After a couple of moments, the waiter returned, carrying their food and drinks and placed them carefully on the table.

"By the way, why do you think Devang Awasthi was killed and that he did not commit suicide?" she asked, serving few pieces of fish on his plate.

"His suicide was just a cooked up story that his family spread to the media," he said, putting a piece of fish in his mouth. "When I reached the crime scene, the first thing that poked my hunch was the projection of that bullet. He was correctly holding his licenced gun in his right hand. If he would have shot his own head, sitting in a wheelchair, either the bullet would have traversed parallel or upwards through his head. But the bullet moved downwards, which can only be possible if someone shoots his head, standing next to him," he explained, forming the shape of a gun with his fingers and making several gestures of shooting his own head. Ahi nodded spellbindingly to his words of observation.

"Now, if that was not a suicide, then who killed him?" he asked and continued after a pause as if he was reframing his words to convey in best possible way, "While I was looking for this answer, I found innumerable faces as suspects who had motives to kill him. In fact, he kept on making enemies throughout his entire lifetime due to his deeds as a member of that notorious syndicate of NCR."

"Yes, I just read about that. So, why don't the police take any action against them?" she asked, disturbed.

Abhimanyu smirked, answering her, "Do you think it's a gang of some street guys? Every member of this syndicate holds a powerful position in our system. They twist, break and rebuild our system for their benefit. Being part of this system, they run a parallel system of their own."

Ahi nodded as she had heard that earlier from her father as well.

"Going by the circumstantial evidence and place, I started my investigation from his family members and frequent visitors first. Because, it was easier for me as well, compared to chasing the members of the syndicate," he said, biting into the chicken wings.

"And you found Maya and Dhruv as the prime suspects because of his property," Ahi added, sipping her drink. He nodded confirming.

Ahi retorted, "Why did Dhruv have to murder his father? He was going to be the sole owner of that entire property after his father died."

"No, this Devang Awasthi was not that simple. I met his lawyer to know about the status of his property and came to know that, he changed his will a day before his murder to donate all his property to an orphanage. So, it's quite possible that Dhruv and Maya tried to stop him before he could change that will, but they missed it by a day."

"Possible," she murmured, thoughtfully.

"The other person of that house was Hari – harmless, old, poor and loyal to his master. I don't see anything suspicious in him. A frequent visitor, his ghost writer, Praveen, a middle-aged, educated and poor guy used to help Devang in typing his scripts. Devang was quite frail and couldn't type on his own in the last few years before his death. Praveen didn't like Devang Awasthi as he used to insult him for minute mistakes, but that can't be the reason to kill anyone. And the last person is his driver, Raghav. He had been working for Devang since the last fifteen years. He would have killed Devang long back if he wanted to. Though, this driver and ghost writer are still under my surveillance," he justified his decision. After a moment, he said excitedly, "A person who cannot type... how could he trigger a gun?"

"Moreover, I have not found any fingerprint or any evidence which can establish the presence of any outsider. Though, no one is so stupid to murder someone without gloves," he continued after recollecting the facts in his mind. "There was no sign of struggle on his body. He did not even try to resist."

"So, you mean to say the killer was someone close to him," she asked.

He confirmed, nodding and said, "Only someone close to him would know where he used to keep his gun. And how could I miss those marks of foundation powder on his right earlobe? That confirms the involvement of a female."

Ahi looked up at him and nodded. "But unfortunately, before I could collect any solid evidence against them, the case was closed, concluding it as a suicide and I was removed from that case," he said shrugging his shoulders.

"Syndicate?" she asked, placing her palm on his hand.

She had grown up witnessing her father's disappointment on many such occasions. She'd embrace her father and whisper close to his ears, "you are my superhero; you can do it". That moment, she wished to hug Abhimanyu in the same way.

"Yeah, someone from syndicate in my department. They don't allow anyone to interfere in any matter of their members to keep their business secret," he said in a low voice.

"I am worried about Hari's wife; she must be miserable now. Can't we help her a bit?" Ahi asked in concern.

"What? Are you serious? As far as I know, he is unmarried."

"But that night, I saw a blouse, a saree and a book on human psychology in his house," she argued, frowning.

"That might be Maya's. She might have given it to him for wash or something. Is it not possible? Not sure about that book though," he asked, being reluctant to make the scene more complicated.

"No, I don't think so. Those blouses were way bigger in size with respect to her and I don't think she wears those kind of cheap, glittery and bright sarees."

"That means there is someone else in that house." The wrinkles on Abhimanyu's face were eloquent enough to express his discomfort.

They hung out till late night as Ahi started telling him about Devang Awasthi's life from that manuscript. She thought that might help him in his investigation.

13

After twenty chest-presses, Abhimanyu found it tough to move the handles anymore, as he was completely drained out.

"Yaa!" He shouted, contorting his face, drenched in sweat. The veins bulged beneath the skin of his forearms, chest and shoulder, but he failed to lift the weight-bars. He left the handle, huffing and frowning.

"What the hell is going on man? I can't even reach my lowest rep of one set," he asked his gym instructor in frustration.

"Abhi, this is because of your haphazard lifestyle. You starve the whole day, don't sleep properly. A human needs a minimum of six to eight hours of sleep per day," the trainer informed.

"Tell me about it," Abhimanyu whispered sulkily. "But my city neither allows me to sleep nor gives me ample time to relax. I have been born and brought up in this city and I love this place for the innocence of its inhabitants. But I had never seen those grievous faces behind the mask," he continued in a tired voice.

He sighed and added after a pause, "Or maybe I was innocent then, so did not realize what lay behind those masks."

The trainer smiled compassionately.

"Time's up!" Abhimanyu smirked, receiving a call on his hands-free.

"Sir ji, someone has murdered Dhruv. Quickly come near Jalvayu Vihar in Sector 25," Sharma ji informed.

Abhimanyu was dumbstruck for a few moments before he responded, "I am coming."

He rushed down the gym's hall to reach the men's room.

Ahi read those words printed on that crumpled paper for the fifth time. It was similar to the previous one, wrapped over a small stone to traverse the distance to her window from the street and had those same broken 'T' and 'S'. She glanced at the typewriter placed in the corner of her room and muttered, "But how?"

It read:

Pari was precious to her brothers, more than their own lives. She was the only reason for her mother to smile, bearing all the miseries of her life. They had been trying to be happy in their imperfect life until that demon king arrived.

"What the fuck is it?" she murmured thoughtfully, lighting a cigarette.

She wondered, if the previous message was to help her in publishing this manuscript, then what could be this message be for? How could she find her secret well-wisher, and why was that person not showing up? Was there any other intention beneath that helping gesture to win her trust? Her thoughts were hopping from one question to another as the fire steadily approached the filter of her cigarette, leaving burnt ashes behind.

She was startled by the ring of her mobile.

"Yes Samim," she responded, seeing Samim's name on the screen.

"You didn't even inform me that you have got the signature," he complained disappointedly. Ahi kept quiet, realizing her mistake. Samim continued after a pause, expecting some explanation from her, "I came to know from others that you have sent the signed agreement and scanned copy of that manuscript for editing."

Ahi closed her eyes and frowned, biting her tongue as she said, "I am sorry, Samim."

"Anything better than this?" His voice had a hint of sarcasm.

"Please, don't be mad at me. You can't believe how much pressure there was. It just slipped out of mind," she said in a feeble tone. "See, I am saying sorry, making a puppy face," she said pouting as she did not get any response from him.

"So, when are you coming back? Or is that something you can't share with me?"

"Come on yaar! I am sorry," she pleaded. After a few mute moments, she added, "It might take a few more days for me to wrap all the things here. I have to help a friend of mine who actually helped to get this signature."

"Oh really! Is he that super cop?" Samim asked promptly.

"Oh, my goodness, are you guys twin sisters? I mean you and Maa, just can't breathe without sharing any tiny information about me with you," she said, giggling.

"What's his name, by the way?" he asked, evading her jest.

"Abhimanyu Rathore... ACP," she answered. There was no response from his side.

"You know what, he is a big fan of Baba. I just get tired answering his questions about my father and his questions are so stupid and funny. And he is..." she continued laughing, but before she finished her words, Samim remarked, "Nice trick."

"What trick?" she jumped on his word.

"Trick to hang out with a girl, portraying himself as innocent."

"Come on Samim, you hardly know his name. How can you judge someone like this?" she snapped back in irritation.

"Exactly how you are quarrelling with me for a person you hardly know," Samim retorted.

An unconscious sense stitched their lips. Ahi heard a few beeps in her mobile. She glanced its screen to find Abhimanyu's call on wait. She placed the mobile back on her ear, ignoring his call.

Abhimanyu kept his mobile back into his pocket, not getting any response from Ahi and started gazing at Dhruv's corpse. The smashed forehead, including a portion of the left eye-hole distorted Dhruv's face, making it almost unidentifiable. The body lay prone on the street in a black jacket and jeans. The legs were slightly apart; the right leg straight and the left leg bent at the hip and knee. The left arm was bent and slightly under the body with the hand approximately one inch from the face. The right arm was extended perpendicular to the body and bent at the elbow. As if he had tried to get his gun which was lying on the street, slightly away from his reach. Blood was splattered all over the street from his crushed head and flowed towards the body, following the slope of the street. The murder weapon, a large stone, was thrown by the roadside and was partly covered in fresh blood and smashed internal organs beneath the human skull.

"Dubey ji, arrange some more force, we can't restrict this crowd," Abhimanyu ordered loudly, pointing to the cumulative crowd around that area. Dubey nodded. Chaddha was busy with the photographer to capture every minute details of the crime scene.

"What do you think, Sharma ji?" Abhimanyu asked, sitting on his haunches by the corpse.

"The victim strongly fought against the killer. As you see, other than that fatal injury on his head, there are lots of other injuries all over his body," senior constable Sharma said, carefully observing the corpse.

"Hmm…And his left knee is broken badly. So, he might have crawled on the street to reach his gun there. But before he could grasp his weapon, the killer smashed his head with that mammoth stone and threw it there," Abhimanyu described as if he was visualizing that incident in front of his eyes, pointing at all the evidence.

"Sir, in that case, the back of his head should have been injured, not the forehead," Sharma retorted.

"The victim might have turned his head to check the position of the killer," Abhimanyu explained inattentively, leaning on the stagnant blood around the waist of the cadaver. He frowned, staring at the blood as he wore the glove on his right hand.

"Sharma ji, get me the forceps," he ordered, extending his gloved palm.

"What is this?" Abhimanyu asked, holding a thin, arc-shaped glass piece by the forceps. He shook the forceps gently to get rid of the blood on it. It glittered, reflecting the ray of the sun as soon as the blood dripped off from its surface.

"Glass bangle," both of them said in a chorus. Abhimanyu called a forensic-officer and ordered him to collect any other such pieces of a bangle around that area.

"I am quite sure that this murder is an act of revenge and not sure why I am comfortable to presume the killer as a female. It was not a planned murder and done in the heat of the moment. Otherwise, the killer should have carried some kind of weapon for sure," Abhimanyu said, thoroughly scanning that area.

"Should we check Hari's family background?" Sharma asked, catching the hint in Abhimanyu's words.

Abhimanyu turned back to him, smiled and teased, "Wow, are you eating walnuts every day?"

"Sir, *aap bhi na*," Sharma said, shy and abashed.

"But two things bother me about the theory of a female killer; one of them is that heavy stone. Is it possible for a female to lift that stone and throw it in a particular direction?" Abhimanyu wondered.

Sharma nodded thoughtfully and asked, "What is the second one?"

"This place," he answered, sighing and added after a pause, "Sharma ji, this is an open street, countless people are walking on it every day. So, there is no guarantee that the piece of bangle belongs to the killer. They might be scattered on this street long before."

In the meanwhile, that forensic expert informed Abhimanyu that he had found few pieces of glass bangles; few of them are of the same colour and few are of different colours. Abhimanyu ordered him to collect as much evidence as possible as they could not block that street for an entire day. He pulled out his mobile and called Ahi once again.

"Hello Ahi, are you fine?" he asked impatiently immediately after she picked the call.

"Yes. Why? What happened? Is everything all right?" she asked concerned.

"If you are safe, then it is all right as of now. I was worried as you didn't pick up the phone in the morning," he said in relief. "Dhruv has been brutally murdered last night. Someone smashed his head with a giant stone," he added.

"Oh god! What is going on?" Her voice reflected her fear.

"If I listen to my gut feeling, it's a revenge for Hari's murder, and in that case, you too should be on the killer's radar. So, just keep me posted about what is happening around you and try to stay at home," he warned.

In the meanwhile, a boy handed a cup of tea in his hand and rushed to the other officers to serve them the tea.

"I just found another crumpled paper in my room, similar to that previous one I told you about and I have a clue about those weird lines written on it," she informed, gazing at that piece of paper.

"Okay, I will drop by your place to see that; may be in the afternoon or in the evening sometime after wrapping up this mess. Stay safe, keep your door locked and don't open it for any unknown person," he said.

"Okay," she assured before hanging up.

He kept the phone in his pocket, wondering about the next step of the killer and took a sip of the tea. All of a sudden, he frowned in anger and shouted, "What the hell is going on, Dubey ji? We can't drink tea at a crime scene. It can just ruin evidence if someone spills it over here." A silence overpowered all the chitchat of those officers around. "Look at that boy, he is just running bare feet all over the area," he hollered, came out of the crime scene in frustration, walked down on the street a little far off and lit a cigarette.

His mobile vibrated in his pocket.

"Yes, sir," he responded, drawing his mobile out of his pocket.

"What the hell is going on, Abhi? We have to find and shoot the killer immediately before the situation goes out of our hand. Take it as my unofficial order. I don't want this killer opening his mouth in court or anywhere. Is that clear?" a heavy male voice asked.

"I got it, sir," he replied politely.

"And remember that we are looking for a promotion, because you can help our group more effectively."

"Yes, sir." A smile of desire and aggression lit up Abhimanyu's face.

Being compelled to stay inside the locked doors of that flat, Ahi started reading the manuscript.

Almost a month had passed since that night, there was no such news which could alert me until that morning when a policeman arrived at my home. He snatched all my drowsiness as I saw him in my backward along with my driver and Radha. After a small interrogation, he headed towards the main entrance as Radha's mute gestures could not help him much. I rushed down the stairs, ran past the hall to reach the lawn.

"What's the matter, officer?" I asked, carefully governing my over-curiosity and pondering expression. I lengthened the span of my breathing to normalize the panting which helped me to pretend my presence over there as a mere coincident.

The policeman turned back and greeted me with a smile, "Good morning sir!" My driver followed him.

"Good morning officer. May I help you?"

"I don't think so," he replied, taking off his cap and continued. "Radha's husband has been reported missing last night. So we are just checking all possible places."

"Must be lying somewhere on the road, bloody drunkard," my driver Raghav blurted. The wrinkles of disgust ran over his face which could not escape the eyes of the policeman. Raghav evolved as an escape for me if in case I required one as his manifestation of anger for Radha's husband smelled like a motive.

"The person who reported him missing met him around a couple of months back and they came here to meet Radha that night," the policeman informed, gazing at Raghav.

"Oh really! Then, I believe, you might start your investigation from that very moment when he returned from here," I said, cleaning the glasses of my specs. It was quite soothing to me that the investigation, started on a misguided foundation and could never reach me and I might not need to sacrifice innocent Raghav.

"Correct, but it is next to impossible. Everyone has something better to do than notice an insignificant man like him and remember all the minute details of an ordinary day of his life," the policeman said, hopelessly.

"Hmm… then you should look for the motives," I advised, wearing a mask of his pseudo well-wisher.

"Sir, you won't believe, I didn't find a single person till now who likes him, including that man who has reported the case. But, Radha should be benefited the most," he informed, smirking and added after a thoughtful mute moment, "I would rather prefer to close this case than arrest her if my investigation points at her by any means. I know this couple since years and have arrested him several times before for domestic violence."

I nodded, appreciating his perception.

These words on these pages are just perfectly arranged wooden logs of my pyre; they are only deprived of the touch of holy fire as no second person knows about these pages. However, I cannot help writing them as my typewriter and these sheets of paper are the only things I can believe in. I have earned money, fame, respect, power, and connections, but not a living entity to trust. I hope these pages never come to anyone's notice, even after my death, and to ensure that, I have decided to burn them after emptying my heart and mind.

I never want people to read about a monster just to mislay faith on humanity. Monsters, demons, devils or whatever they are called, humans are at peace believing that they are some different entities, identifiable contrastingly as non-human. But in reality, they reside among humans and resemble only humans.

The demon inside me was satisfied to watch his angel every day, unshackled, governing her life on her own terms and wishes, soaring around with a mesmerizing smile and glow on her face. She was unaware of her husband's demise, but she realized his incapability to torture her at least for a few days. Her innocent heart beguiled, absorbing each drop of that uncertain happiness which she believed to be finished abruptly.

Normally, she used to wait for my return at the dining table. Howsoever late at night it might be, she ensured my dinner was served hot and fresh. Moreover, she used to attend to me till I finished my dinner. But, that night, dinner was served on the table before my arrival. I placed my office's stuff in their proper places, took off my formals and stood under the warm shower. It always rejuvenated me. I put on my bathrobe, coming out of the shower and returned to the dining table, hoping for her presence that time. Still, she was not there. I searched for her in all the possible places inside the bungalow, including Dhruv's rooms. He was not at home either.

I rushed to her outbuilding at the backyard, abandoning the dinner on the table, just to confirm that she was safe and secure. The door opened partly, noisily, as I hesitantly pushed it gently with my fingers.

"Radha!" I called in a low voice, before plunging myself into the darkness of that room. I pushed my reluctant feet on the floor as I did

not hear any response. I stood there like a statue for a few moments, leaving the door open, allowing my eyes sometimes to adapt to the darkness.

Radha lay on a thin mattress on the floor as her asleep kids left no space for her on that narrow cot. I knelt down on the floor by the mattress and whispered, "Radha," tapping her on her hand gently. She moaned, moving her hand away. Her slovenly wrapped saree was displaced, partially exposing her red blouse and petticoat in different places. I placed my palm on her forehead and felt her body temperature was quite high; she was burning. She grabbed my hand as I attempted to stand.

"You will be absolutely fine. Let me bring some medicine for you," I whispered, leaning my face close to hers.

She wrapped her right arm around my neck, tugged me hastily and pressed her lips hard on mine. Her soft, wet and warm lips opened, brushing all over my face before returning to my lips again. She sucked my lower lip, bit it gently before her tongue caressed it. She stroked her tongue inside my mouth, deep, greedy for more of me, all of me. She was in a hurry, as if the delayed gratification smashed the barrier of her tolerance. She rose, smoothly pushing me down on the mattress, letting her saree to slide down from her shoulder. She rode on me, revealing her deep cleavage over that tight, red blouse as I lay down. She tugged open the knot of my bathrobe, unclothed me and flung herself on me like a rain of warm water. I was melting beneath the warmth of her body, savouring the unaltered, raw smell of her skin that was more captivating than any artificial perfume. She spread kisses all over my chest, sometimes with gentle bites and sometimes with deep sucks, portraying the misery of her life on the canvas of my body. I allowed her to do whatever she wished to, laying on that mattress like her prey to bring a bit of equivalence in her sexually tortured past. I was mentally prepared to get her a chance to satiate her maliciousness of sexual revenge, torturing me, a male body. Though her foreplay was not agonising; it reflected her care and affection for me.

She stopped her play after a few minutes, moved away from my chest to sit straight on my thighs and stared at me, panting. The dilation of that pair of pupils on those bluish green irises of her eyes, the wrinkled skin under her eyes, lifted corner of her lips and widening forehead proclaimed her arousal with dominance. That expression could burn down any male in ecstasy. I sat straight, getting up from the mattress and curved my palm over her cheeks while my thumb caressed the contour of her cheekbone. I felt her wet private part on my thigh as I softly nibbled her upper lip. She closed her eyes in immense pleasure. I grabbed her throat, gently kissing her forehead, cheeks, eyes, ears and jawlines. My palm slid down on her breast from her throat while my lips were busy painting some hickeys on her slender, soft and fair neck. She moaned softly. I pulled her hard against me, grabbing her fleshy but firm butt-cheeks. She started rubbing her private part on mine, moaning and exhaling heavily. I pushed my hand hard inside her blouse, tearing off a few buttons; they scattered on the floor. Her body was supple enough to arch back on the floor in ecstasy as I firmed my grip on her butts with both of my hands. I rolled my tongue on her clay-lamp shaped deep and dark navel. She stretched her arm down and held my face firmly on her navel, grabbing my hair. The pleasure arrowed through my blood as my fingers ran over her sensuous curved body and reached her breasts. I *released those heavy, soft and bulged out twins tearing apart the rest of the buttons of her blouse. I savoured all the patches, stretch marks, the marks of those dried-out wounds and that small mole at the left of her suprasternal notch, those three on the back of her left shoulder, the hidden one under her right breast, the bigger and pale one on the inner side of her left thigh. I sipped on them at the long planes and sinewy curves of her body. I explored and mapped her until I learnt which spot made her whimper, made her moan, quiver, arch in ecstasy while her nails dug into my skin. I discovered everything about her as I felt she was just a complementing part of my body, carrying those similar wounds of mine, only diverse in feminine attributes.*

Those words turned on Ahi. She touched herself, closing her eyes, but opened them wide the very next moment, startled to have envisioned Abhimanyu.

A hi spent almost forty-five minutes in front the mirror before settling herself in an little black dress with spaghetti straps, a pair of diamond stud earrings and a choker necklace with a diamond locket. She touched up her face with a light foundation to hide the dark circles around her eyes, applied a little gloss on her lips, took her black clutch and put on her black stilettos before leaving the apartment.

She blushed as she approached the ground floor, walking down the stairs. She didn't remember the last time she had dressed up. She was not clear about her feeling for Abhimanyu, but she liked to hang out with him and she always felt secure when he was around.

"Wow!" Abhimanyu reacted as soon as she came out on the road from her apartment.

It was almost 10 p.m. when Abhimanyu called her after wrapping up his work for the day. He wanted to meet her at her place, just to see the suspicious pieces of paper. But, Ahi chose to hang out somewhere outside as there was an unusual chance that her uncle could spend that night at his home.

"I should have worn something better in that case," he mocked her, pointing at his casual shirt and jeans. "Don't you think, you are making it difficult for me to behave like a decent man?" he asked, coquettishly.

"Oh, is it? I thought I am going out for dinner with a decent IPS officer," she teased, dramatically caressing her short hair. She glanced at his face from the corner of her eyes as he looked away, running out of words. "Sooo, I thought, I am in the safest hands to wear anything I want," she concluded, concealing her smile under a concerned face.

He smiled, brooded in the mischievousness of her sea-greenish pair of eyes and said after a few moments while gazing into her eyes, "By the way, where are we going tonight?"

"We will go to Owlcity."

"No, I don't like pubs or disco kind of stuff. You may think I am backdated or unsmart, but that's the way I am," he protested, frowning and kick-started his bike.

"Will you stop behaving like a grandfather? Owlcity is not anything like that. It is just a restaurant, remains open till 4 a.m. And they have all kinds of Italian and American fast foods," she argued, raising her voice a little louder. "And I am sure, you had nothing other than innumerable cups of tea and cigarettes from those roadside stalls the entire day," she added in a comparatively lower voice.

"Where is it?" His voice melted, observing her concern regarding him.

"Sector nineteen," she replied sullenly as she rode on his backseat. "Huh! I have never seen an IPS officer who doesn't know his own city properly and a Bong girl from another city who knows it better," she teased, placing her hand on his shoulder.

He smiled impishly before driving the bike with a violent jerk. She had to grasp him with both of her arms from the back to sustain her balance on the backseat.

"Hold me tightly, Bong-girl from another city," he said dramatically, turning his face. She smiled, resting her head on the back of his shoulder.

Samim glanced at his wrist watch impatiently as he was trapped inside the flight, waiting for the gate to open. It was 11 p.m.

"Open the damn door man," he whispered, getting irritated at the pilot's announcement to inform the travellers about the outside weather in detail. His flight, which was scheduled to arrive at Indira Gandhi International Airport, New Delhi before 9.30, was late by almost two hours.

The gate opened within the next fifteen minutes while the Airbus came to a standstill. Samim approached the gate in frustration, moving step by step in that sluggish queue of his co-passengers. He did not smile back at the air-hostess as she bid him a pleasant night ahead at the gate of departure and rushed to the baggage carousel assigned for his flight. He groped inside the pocket of his blazer just to confirm the presence of that ring box. He collected his tiny trolley-bag from the belt and rushed to the restroom.

"Uff! Everything is messed up," he muttered to himself finding his messy hair, haphazardly tucked shirt and wrinkles on his linen blazer and trousers in front the wide mirror of the men's room.

He splashed some water on his head, ran his fingers through his hair to arrange it in a presentable manner, tucked his shirt properly, repositioned the tie-knot perfectly in the middle, buttoned the blazer, leaving the last two buttons open and looked at himself in the mirror like a critique. He smiled as he found the person in the mirror quite attractive in that grey linen blazer on a sky-blue shirt and brown tie.

He picked up the luggage and rushed towards the departure gate.

"Hmm…These are from the same typewriter," Abhimanyu commented after scrutinizing the two pieces of paper. "So, all this had been planned long back. Someone typed these lines and then informed you to pick this typewriter from a particular scrap dealer," he continued, gazing at the sheets of paper and whispered, "But why?"

"To help me publish that manuscript," Ahi retorted.

In the meanwhile, a waiter delivered their food on their table. Ahi ordered three slices of three different pizzas. Abhimanyu ordered some roasted chicken and salad.

"But what could be the motive behind that? And why have you been chosen for that purpose? How the hell does someone know about a girl from Kolkata?" he asked himself, more than her. He nibbled on a chicken piece, dipping it in the garlic sauce. Ahi smiled pointing at the droplet of sauce, dripping on his chin from the lower lip.

"What?" he asked, confused. She stretched her arm, leaning on the table and rubbed her thumb on his lip and chin, cleaning the sauce. He lost himself for a few moments as the feathery touch of her soft palm tickled his lips.

"Sauce," she replied. "By the way, you were saying something about a girl from far Kolkata," she added, noticing his bewildered eyes, touching the unclothed portions of her body for the first time since she met him.

"Yes... I... I am not getting the motive behind all these," he fumbled, taking his eyes away from her as he realized their boisterousness.

Somehow, Samim managed a to get a cab that was ready to drop him at sector twenty-six, Noida as he agreed to pay almost double than the normal charge.

"How long will it take to reach there?" he asked after settling himself on the back seat carefully to avoid any more wrinkles on his blazer or trousers.

"It takes a little more than an hour in normal traffic," the driver replied.

Samim grinned like an idiot, failing to conceal the boiling excitement inside him to meet Ahi as his cab started rushing on the airport road.

"Basically, this manuscript is a candid confession of Devang Awasthi, something he had never wanted to publish. That's quite normal for anyone," Abhimanyu said thoughtfully, as if he was trying to connect some dots to get to a conclusion. "So, whoever is trying to publish this manuscript, wants to defame Devang Awasthi," he whispered. Ahi nodded in agreement.

"But still… why you and why after two months of his death? Why will someone put so much of effort to defame a dead person? And you are all set to publish this manuscript now; then what else does this person want from you? What's the meaning of this second slip?" The frustration was vivid in his voice.

"Hey, it's okay; don't be so stressed out," she consoled, caressing his hand with her fingers. He gave a blank stare. "You know what, whenever I see my father worried and stressed out after returning from his duty, I cuddle him, sitting on his lap, and within a few seconds, his all problems evaporate in the air." She could not help spilling out her thought.

He smiled, gazing at her mesmerising pair of eyes. "My cuddle has a magical spell," she told him, shrugging her shoulders with a lot of flamboyance.

Abhimanyu's mobile rang, making a shrill noise of vibration on that wooden table.

"Yes, Chaddha ji," he responded, receiving the call.

"Our Hari had a restaurant in Paharganj, called Haridwar. But he had sold it to someone else a few years back, which is strange to me," Chaddha informed.

"Why strange?"

"Because this restaurant was quite famous in that locality and used to earn him a lot of profit. Sir, why would someone sell a profiting business just to work as a servant?"

"Hmm… Good going, Chaddha ji. Carry on your investigation and keep informing me about your findings. I will be available the entire night; just give me a call at any time," Abhimanyu instructed before disconnecting.

"Hari was the owner of a small restaurant in Paharganj… Haridwar," he said, reading the unasked question in Ahi's eyes.

"I read about this place in this script. As far as I remember, this was the restaurant where Radha's husband used to go for lunch and dinner all the time," Ahi said excitedly.

"That means Hari had some other intention while working in Awasthi Nivas. If Hari killed Devang, then who is that lady leaving her traces in all the crime locations," he whispered to himself. "I need your help to know each and every word of this manuscript as quickly as possible. Don't know why, but I feel the killer is hidden in those pages," he said impatiently. Ahi's eyes glittered in enthusiasm to be a part of his investigation and she nodded like an obedient kid.

"I believe, all these incidents are connected to each other. Hari's entry in Awasthi Niwas as a servant, Devang Awasthi's murder, those marks of foundation-powder on Devang's right earlobe, your involvement in publishing this manuscript, these slips in your room, Dhruv's murder, those broken bangles, that invisible strong lady who could lift that heavy stone and Haridwar – all of these are connected. We just need to find that missing link," he continued, arranging all the events in his mind.

They had to spend a few more minutes waiting for their check and its payment before leaving the restaurant. On the way, back to Ahi's place, Abhimanyu was numb on the surface to respond to Ahi's light talks and kept driving the bike in cold silence. But he was arguing with himself inside his mind, desperate to find the missing link.

Samim got out of his cab as it stopped in front of Jaideep's apartment. He paid the driver and went straight up to the third floor. He took out the ring box from his blazer's pocket, held that in his right hand, opening the lid, rang the doorbell and kneeled down in front of the door.

"Will you marry me?" he whispered, rehearsing his line. But no one opened the door, even after waiting for a few minutes. He rang the doorbell again and waited for a few more moments. After waiting there for some time, he called her up on her mobile.

"Hi Samim, what's up?" Ahi responded in a loud voice, receiving the call as the noisy wind at the backseat of Abhimanyu's bike made it difficult for her to hear anything.

"Aren't you at home? What's the noise?" he enquired.

"No Samim, I came out for dinner and now am on my way back home. I will call you in the next thirty to forty minutes. I can't hear you properly," she replied loudly.

"Okay."

Samim came back to the road, hid behind a tree by that apartment though that alley was dark enough to swallow all the visibility.

After a few minutes, Abhimanyu's bike entered that dark lane and stopped in front of Jaideep's apartment. Ahi stepped down from the bike as Abhimanyu shut the engine.

"Am I privileged to have that magical spell?" he asked whisperingly. Ahi smiled with a lingering shyness on her face.

She moved closer to him as he stood on the road, getting off from his bike. "Isn't it risky on this open road?"

He laughed softly, caressing her jawline and said, "I can't even see you in this darkness. Whom are you expecting to see us?"

She wrapped her arms around his waist. He embraced her firmly and whispered to her ear, "Yes, it's really magical."

She giggled, pressing her breast on his tough abdomen and rested her head on his wide masculine chest. They spent a few minutes in each other's arms, savouring the curves of each other's bodies.

Samim's vision blurred as tears welled up. The darkness failed to hide Ahi from him. He stood there like a statue, witnessing his dream scattering to pieces. It started drizzling. Few drops fell on his blazer which he was carrying delicately since that morning. However, he did not mind.

Some drops fell on Ahi's face and lips. Abhimanyu drank them one by one from her face and nibbled her lower lips tenderly. She pressed her lips on his upper lip. They started kissing each other insanely.

"Enough, this is a road," Ahi whispered, gathering her senses back. She stepped on his boot. Her stilettos helped her to raise herself up to his face and she kissed his forehead. "See you tomorrow. Bye," she whispered and ran inside the apartment. Abhimanyu drove away.

It started raining heavily. Samim sat under that tree, weeping inconsolably. The man who had been lighting the faces of Kolkata's people with smiles had no one to wipe his tears other than those droplets of rain.

15

"Sir, that junky has confessed that Dhruv gave him money to murder Hari," Chaddha informed right after Abhimanyu stepped inside the police station the next morning.

"That was expected," Abhimanyu said indifferently, approaching his cabin. Chaddha followed him.

"So, one murder is resolved. But, this Hari was not as innocent as we are assuming," Abhimanyu stated, lounging himself on his chair and gestured to Chaddha to take the chair placed at the other side of his table.

"Thank you, sir," Chaddha said, occupying a chair.

"Let's revisit all the suspects," Abhimanyu proposed, pushing his chair back to get a comfortable position.

Chaddha nodded and continued, "First and prime suspect was Dhruv with the motive of owning all the assets of his father before his father could give them to someone else."

"Next."

"Next is Maya, a poor young widow... had relationships with several young and rich men before marrying Devang Awasthi, who was fifteen years older than her. Their marriage is more like a business deal."

"Hmm... securing her shelter, food and lavish lifestyle in exchange of sexually satisfying an old man," Abhimanyu added.

"Yes, and the motive is same, Devang's property."

"Are we not looking at only one side of a coin? In fact, we have never flipped the other side of this coin."

"What do you mean?" Chaddha asked enthusiastically.

"Though the circumstantial evidence always led us to Dhruv and Maya. And it's quite convenient to think that they might have killed Devang for his property before Devang could change his will, unaware of the fact that he had given it to some orphanage. But isn't it possible that someone murdered him to stop any further change to that will?"

Chaddha nodded and said, "That must be someone from that orphanage then. But we have already talked to all the suspects and neither of them are from that orphanage."

"Chaddha ji, people lie," Abhimanyu said, smiling and abandoned his chair abruptly. "Let's go."

Ahi had been riffling through that manuscript since morning from a different perspective in her mind. Hence, those following pages where the author had described the most soothing days of his life when he and Radha had been basking a fairy tale, in reality, seemed unimportant to her. She was rushing through those romantic phases to stumble on that next incident which could throw some light on the darkness of Abhimanyu's investigation.

We were not a necessity to each other anymore; rather became each other's desire. A person always tries to bind their relationship with some name, according to our society that only turns the relationship in a rigorous obligation. Neither I nor Radha was bothered to define our relationship. We were happy to keep it undefined, unnamed, untidy and unshackled, only to float on our mutual craving, pleasure, and warmth of our skins.

However, that curse of life did not show any mercy on me this time as well. It found an excuse to take her away from me; only because I had started dreaming of growing old and dying in her lap.

It was an ordinary summer evening. Just after sunset, the land and water bodies had just started releasing the heat they had absorbed through the day. That increased the temperature of the air exponentially. Radha loved to be seduced by the touch of ice cubes during that period of time. It was a treat to my eyes, watching her moaning in pleasure and exhaling in ecstasy while the ice melted over her quivering curves, absorbing the heat of her body.

That evening, she substituted our roles in that summer foreplay. She rode on me, holding an ice-cube between her teeth and started rubbing it all over my body. Every touch of that ice cube stole the heat beneath my skin. I closed my eyes, savouring those touches. After a couple of minutes, she stopped all of sudden and got off of me hastily. I opened my eyes in curiosity. She stood on the floor, huddling the saree in a frail attempt to cover her body. I looked at her shocked pair of eyes, staring at that open door. I could not see anything, other than a swiftly passing shadow who was witnessing our foreplay till that very moment.

I never came to know who that person was, but that small shadow was dark and large enough to overcast my soothing days in Radha's arms. She was not comfortable with me anymore after that evening and started avoiding me. I had to spend days in unilateral desire as she was reluctant to even sit close to me. And one morning a few months later, she left me forever as I found her lifeless body on her floor. She had committed suicide, poisoning herself. She had poisoned her son before her death. She might have thought that there won't be anyone to take care of her retarded and handicapped son after her death, and I believe, she was absolutely correct. Her infant daughter was playing with her own fingers, lying by the corpse of her elder brother on the bed. Her innocent giggling manifested the belief of her mother in humanity. Even after that miserable life, Radha had believed someone, maybe me, to raise her daughter. Unfortunately, I had no courage to restore her trust as I was already a failure as a father.

Today, after several years of her death, I realize that she might have been ashamed of having a physical relation with me in front of that person who witnessed our foreplay that evening. Isn't it strange of human behaviour? We are not ashamed of torturing ourselves to carry some rotten social obligations in the name of relations. But, we are ashamed of that reason which makes us happy, breaking those ridiculous convictions and rules of our society. She was like that flame of a lamp which burns the slender wick, absorbing even the last drop of oil, leaving only a blackened wick and a thin trace of smoke behind.

The investigation officer who was handling that case was honest and intelligent, quite a rare combination I had seen. He stretched the case for a longer period until all the evidence convinced him that the incident was pure suicide. He was a good human being too. He had taken all the responsibility of the rehabilitation of that infant in an orphanage, Ashiana.

I envied that police officer for his qualities that I always craved for: honesty, courage, humanity, and responsibility. I wished he could help me to raise Dhruv, as unlike me, he had all those ingredients to be an ideal father.

Ahi flipped the page with tears in her eyes. She picked up her mobile to see any notification from Samim. She had been trying to reach him since she reached home the previous night, but failed, as his mobile was switched off since then. She called up his number once again, not finding any notification from him either, just to get the same result.

"Fuck you, man." She threw her mobile on the bed in irritation.

"Chaddha ji, is it not that orphanage Devang Awasthi's lawyer was talking about?" Abhimanyu asked as their jeep reached in front of an orphanage at sector 35.

"Yes sir, Ashiana. But what are we looking for here?" Chaddha asked, puzzled from the back seat.

"Whether any of our suspects have any connection with this orphanage or not." Abhimanyu hopped out of the jeep and rushed towards the entrance. Chaddha followed him.

They directly entered the front office, crossing that large playground in front of that three-storied main building. Many kids of different ages were playing on the ground.

The old woman at the front office stood up, abandoning the chair in shock to see Chaddha's uniform and asked, "What happened? Any problem?"

"Nothing aunty, please have a seat," Abhimanyu calmed her down, occupying a chair at the other side of her large table. She sat back on her chair reluctantly, glancing at their faces several times alternatively.

"Aunty, I will tell you a few names. You just need to let us know whether you know any of them," Abhimanyu asked, coating her words with extra politeness to make her relaxed and stable. She nodded hesitatingly.

"Devang Awasthi, Maya Awasthi, Dhruv Awasthi, Hari Parashar, Praveen Kumar and Raghav Dixit," Chaddha said in one breath, standing behind Abhimanyu's chair. Pin drop silence overwhelmed that office room as their eyes glued on her mute and perplexed face, waiting for her answer.

"I… I know the Awasthi family," she fumbled, answering.

"How?" Abhimanyu jumped on the next question, leaning on the table.

"Pra… Praveen used to work there. He told me about Devang Awasthi's murder and his family," she stammered, sweating.

"How is he related to this orphanage? I mean, why does he come here?"

"He is an orphan. His parents died in a car accident and his grandparents were too old to take care of an infant. So, being compelled by fate, they had to bring him here. They too passed away many years back," she said emotionally, without fumbling.

"Where can we find him?" Abhimanyu asked, leaving the chair.

"Sir, he is an honest man… educated, kind, hardworking and helpful," she informed, voluntarily.

"Where is he?" Abhimanyu rephrased his question.

"Believe me, sir, he can't do anything wrong," she pleaded, joining her palms.

"He should not have lied to us, that he has no connection with this orphanage while we had been interrogating him after Devang Awasthi's murder. I don't think he is as innocent as you think. It will be better for you to let us know where we can find him now," Abhimanyu said firmly and admonished, "Anyway, we will catch him someday. But you will be in trouble unnecessarily for not cooperating with our investigation."

"He should be in the auditorium at the back of this building," she almost whispered, reluctantly.

They hurried towards the auditorium. The building had an L-shaped, two-storied extended part at the back. That portion of the building was different from the main building, with respect to the structure, colour, and age. It seemed that the two-storied building had been constructed recently. They went into a large hall with a stage at one corner and the rest of the portion occupied with innumerable seats, arranged in rows.

"Wow, isn't it too much for an orphanage which runs on donations?" Abhimanyu asked. Chaddha nodded.

"But I don't see Praveen here; that aunty must have lied, sir," Chaddha said after glancing at all the faces present in that hall.

Some of them were acting on the stage and a few of them were instructing those actors from the chairs.

"He is right there on the stage. Can you see the lady?" Abhimanyu said in a low voice, leaning his face close to Chaddha's ear. Chaddha nodded like a confused kid.

"That is Praveen in a woman's attire and makeover. Shit man! How could I miss this fact, that a man can turn into a woman?" Abhimanyu regretted, clenching his fist.

"Let's catch him." Chaddha started approaching the stage with great enthusiasm, but Abhimanyu pulled him back, grasping his hand, and ordered to wait until their rehearsal finished. They occupied two chairs. From the conversation between the perfectionist director and his actors, Abhimanyu and Chaddha learned that they were playing a portion of the Ramayana; the part where Rama returned to Ayodhya after Ravana's death. Praveen was playing Sita; they must have had scarcity of female actress. The audience applauded to appreciate Praveen's feministic dialogue as he delivered that three-minute-long monologue, satisfying the director on his fourth attempt.

"Bah-bah! You just slapped on those female actresses who has refused to act on our low budget," one man in the audience shouted.

"Undoubtedly, Praveen is the best actor among us. No one had that courage to take up a female's role. Finally, he agreed; he did not want to ruin the very first show," the man who was sitting just in front of Abhimanyu told the other person adjacent to him.

"Yes, he has that passion for art and this orphanage. I heard that he only donated all the money to build this auditorium. He wants to form a team of actors and actresses to help this orphanage," the other person replied, being generous to add a few more words of appreciation for Praveen.

Abhimanyu was listening to their conversation from behind and picked the phrase 'donated all the money to build this auditorium', strengthening his suspicion about Praveen. He exchanged a glance with Chaddha, smiling.

The rehearsal ended in another thirty minutes and Praveen approached the only exit. Abhimanyu and Chaddha followed him.

"Praveen," Abhimanyu called as soon they came out of the hall.

He turned back, had a glance at their faces and started running. Abhimanyu ran behind him like a cheetah had found its prey. Chaddha's bulged out tummy made his life tougher as he started jogging behind them, but he did not need to continue his lope for more than a couple of minutes as Praveen fell down, stumbling over his saree.

"Get up!" Abhimanyu ordered reaching him. He raised himself from the ground, slowly transforming his weight on his arms. It was difficult to identify him as a man in that wig, face paint, ornaments, blouse, and saree.

"I did not do anything, sir; please believe me. I was just his ghost-writer," he pleaded. In the meanwhile, Chaddha reached them panting.

"Then, why are you making us run?" Chaddha asked, huffing. Anger was vivid in his face.

"I was scared, sir. I just want to stay away from police, murder, and this chaos." The droplets of his sweat gliding down on his face melted the face-paint.

"In that case, you shouldn't have lied to us, man; that you have no connection with this orphanage, Ashiana," Abhimanyu retorted, rubbing out a portion of the paint from his face and examining it, smashing the dust in his pinch.

"Because I knew that he had donated all his property to Ashiana, which would make me the prime suspect. I thought that small lie would help to get me rid of all these. I had stopped coming here since his murder. I'm here just for this play," he explained to justify his deed.

"And what do you think? Why would he have chosen only Ashiana to donate all his property?" Abhimanyu enquired, grasping his hand.

"That… that I am not sure about. He had never dis… discussed all that with me," Praveen fumbled, answering as Abhimanyu pushed away all his bangles from his wrist towards the elbow. Praveen continued with his fumbles, "I… I think his son… could have murdered him. I have seen his son and wife threaten him several times for property.

"How did you get this injury?" Abhimanyu asked, pointing the wound on his right wrist and ignored his volunteered statement.

"This happened a few days back while decorating that stage inside the auditorium," he replied promptly.

"What is your relation with Hari Parashar?" Chaddha asked, catching Abhimanyu's intention.

"He is Devang Awasthi's domestic help. That's all I know about him."

"Where did you get the money to build this auditorium?" Abhimanyu asked, gazing into his eyes.

"Devang sir gave it to me when he came to know about my acting skills and my dreams," he replied promptly.

"Then you became greedy when you came to know about his will and killed him. Wasn't it quite easy for you to know where he used to keep his gun and hide in these woman's clothes?" Abhimanyu asked, grasping the neck of his blouse.

"No, I didn't do it. Do you have any proof?" he asked, shaking off Abhimanyu's hand.

"You may go as of now, Mr Sita. But, don't dare to leave the city. Always remember one thing, that you can never hide from me," Abhimanyu admonished him. He nodded before departing.

"Why did you let him go, sir? We could have arrested him," Chaddha asked confusingly while returning to their jeep.

"Face paint, woman's attire, wound on his wrist, Devang's will, Ashiana and his money to build this auditorium – all these are just making him a promising suspect, but not more than that. He can easily get away with it if we arrest him now. Appoint someone to keep him under surveillance. I need each and every minute detail of his activity from now," Abhimanyu ordered. Chaddha nodded.

Abhimanyu pulled his phone out of his pocket as it started ringing. "Hey, Ahi! Good Morning," he greeted.

"Good morning, handsome!" Ahi replied, seductively.

"Hey, can I call you after some time? I am in the middle of something."

"Wow! You are reluctant to talk to your girlfriend who is not even twenty-four hours old. Bored so soon?" she teased, concealing her giggling.

"No yaar! You are taking it all wrong," Abhimanyu said, perplexed.

"Listen, I have an information for you. Radha's daughter was given to an orphanage. What was the name? Yes, Ashiana," she informed. Abhimanyu stopped walking as all his calculations got messed up with that tiny piece of information.

"Huh! Go and stay busy at work all the time," Ahi replied in pseudo anger melodramatically and disconnected the phone as he did not respond.

"What happened, sir?" Chaddha asked as Abhimanyu seemed immensely confused, standing in the middle of that ground like a statue.

"Devang had his own motive to donate his property to this orphanage in particular. Though that doesn't make Praveen innocent, it changes the calculation a bit. If Praveen murdered Devang for his property, then who is that person, trying to defame him even after his death? It seems like all these answers are in front of my eyes. They are teasing me, mocking me, but I am failing to connect them."

"Whaaayy," Ahi screamed, gazing at the ceiling with a contorted face on her fifteenth failed attempt to reach Samim. She called her mother to know his whereabouts.

"Is everything fine, Ahi?" her mother asked, accepting the call after the fourth ring.

"No Maa, Samim's phone is switched off since last night. He called me yesterday when I was out for dinner. So I told him that I will call him back after reaching home. But since then, his mobile is switched off. Do you know anything?" Ahi expressed her concern in a single breath.

"Oh! So that's that reason you remembered me. I knew something must be unusual." Her voice had a sentimental tone.

"Maa, don't be so melodramatic. I call you often. Listen now, if he calls you anytime, just let him know that I am badly expecting his call."

"Hmm… Tomorrow is Shashti, so, please wear a new dress. If you don't have any, buy a new one and attend the *bodhon* in the evening at least," her mother requested.

"Okay. Don't worry, I will go to this Durga pandal adjacent to Jaideep uncle's apartment."

Ahi hung up. She remained brooding about Samim, wondering what was up.

16

The evening aarti of bodhon had already started when Ahi reached the puja-pandal. She had to visit the nearest shopping mall to buy a new churidar, then bought few sweets to offer to Maa Durga. A gratifying smile lit her face as she stepped into the hypnotic atmosphere. The typical face of Maa Durga with her beautiful large and elongated pair of eyes, the third eye on her forehead just under the vermilion on the partition of her curly hair and her sharp nose above the petal like lips had a majestic appearance beneath the drape of smoke from *dhunachi* (incense burner used for the religious ritual in which light and scented smoke are offered to deities) stared at her.

Ahi always thought that a Durga idol represents not only the victory of good over evil, but also the strength of femininity. Though that avatar of Maa Durga with her ten hands, holding nine different weapons and one lotus, had been visualised and constructed in some ancient age, but still, it stood for most things that are relevant even in modern days. Specially, that half bloomed lotus in her hand which symbolises that though success is certain, yet it is not final; the sword symbolises knowledge; *sudarshan chakra* symbolises that the world is controlled by her, a woman, as only a woman can give birth to a human.

Ahi had read a book about Hindu rituals a few days back, and learnt that as a historical practice, puja in Hinduism, had been modelled around the idea of hosting a deity as an honoured and dearest guest in the best way one can, given one's resources, and receiving their happiness and blessings in return. She had learnt about those sixteen offerings which are common in all types of pujas. She moved a little closer to that stage where the Durga idol was placed to check all the offerings. She had fun glancing over the puja arrangement to find those offerings – *pushpa* (flowers), *vastra* (clothes), *dipa* (lamp), *dhupa* (incense), *naivedya* (foods such as cooked rice, fruit, clarified butter, sugar, and betel leaf), *upaveeda* (the sacred thread), etc. She handed over the packet of sweets to the priest who was busy in arranging all the offerings from the devotees.

The priest started chanting the mantras accompanied with the sacred sounds of bell and *dhaak* (a huge membranophone instrument).

"Let me know all the truth, wiping all the darkness away," Ahi whispered, closing her eyes and bringing her palms together.

After few pondering moments of communication with her own soul, she felt a gentle pat on her left thigh. She looked down to find a little boy with messy hair in a torn, dirty shirt and shorts. He smiled at her.

"Cho cute," Ahi muttered, caressing his head.

She pressed his hands together to make his palms touch and closely positioned them in front of his chest. Then she gestured him to close his eyes. In the very next moment, he put his hands down, widely opening his eyes and smiled at her. She glowered her eyes to show her disapproval, but failed to hold that expression for long, looking at that little boy; she smiled back. The boy brought out a folded piece of paper from his pocket and held that in front of her. She took it from him in an impulse reaction and unfolded it hurriedly. It read:

When everything was moulding so perfectly like a fairy tale for them, that demon king killed Pari's mother and one of her brothers. King's knight took Pari far away and gradually she became the universe of that knight. Her other brother was left alone.

Ahi looked for that boy, glancing around the crowd, gathered under that marquee, but could not see him anymore. She rushed towards the street, pushing the crowd to make her way out in vain. She called Abhimanyu to inform about the incident.

"Abhi, I got another piece of paper," Ahi informed immediately after he picked the call.

"Is it? Then why didn't he call me?"

"Who?" she asked confusingly, walking away from the marquee.

"I have asked one of my men to watch your apartment all the time. So that we can catch the sender. I don't know what to do with these useless people in my department."

"It's not his fault. This time a little boy gave it to me; no one threw anything through my window," she clarified.

"What? Who was that boy? How old was he?" he enquired, impatiently, loudly.

"I don't know; he might be nine or ten years old. I failed to follow or catch him. He just vanished all of a sudden," she said disappointingly. He kept silent, regretting the missed opportunity. "I am sorry, Abhi. Actually, I was not prepared for this," she added.

"It's not your fault, Ahi," he consoled and added after a thoughtful pause, "It seems my man has been exposed to your secret messenger. I have to call him off."

"Anyway, when are we meeting today?" he asked.

"We will meet tomorrow evening, not today. I want to finish the manuscript first, then only we might get all the answers we are looking for."

"Okay. But I will miss you."

She giggled and said, "Delayed gratification always enhances the pleasure of a meeting."

"What's that?" he asked perplexedly.

"Leave it, it's out of the syllabus for a policeman," she mocked and disconnected the call, blushing.

Ahi took a break to pour some coffee after leafing through several pages of the manuscript. She felt relaxed to see the thin width of the unread pages. However, throughout that span of time, Samim's switched-off mobile kept disturbing her mind. She checked her mobile for his notification in each minute, but in vain.

She lit a cigarette, returning to her room with the coffee. Her eyes fell on those mysterious pieces of paper as she flipped the last page she had read already. Those words sat in deep inside her core as she had read them several times. She had a strong notion that those words were some extended part of one those stories of Devang Awasthi's life as they were from the typewriter, and that mysterious sender who had helped her to publish that manuscript.

"Asha," she whispered, wondering whether Asha was that girl the chits were talking about as she had two brothers like Pari, but what about the rest of the portion. Who is this demon king? There were four guys who raped and killed her. And who is this trustworthy knight of the demon king? The darkness in her mind got more intense with her gradually burning down the cigarette. She started reading the manuscript with a sip of coffee.

Last night, I heard them again, discussing their plan to murder me when I sneaked into Dhruv's room under the cover of darkness, leaving my wheelchair.

The people around me have started believing my disguise of being a handicapped and retarded old man who already has one leg in the pyre, and I should thank my new wheelchair for that. This prop is really helping me to shape my incapacitated avatar. I have appointed a ghost-writer and I am seeking my servant Hari's mercy to push my wheelchair all the time to move around. These practices are turning quite handy for me to convey impuissance to my closest enemies, Dhruv and Maya.

Sometimes, we need to camouflage ourselves under a layer of fragility to make our enemies complacent enough to make mistakes. It is my strategy to defeat the enemies, especially when they are our closest people under the same roof.

"We have to do something," Maya whispered, exhaling as Dhruv pressed her bare breasts from behind. She grasped his hair, passing her fingers through them as he nibbled her neck.

"I will kill him, don't worry," Dhruv assured her.

"But we must do it in a certain way that it looks like a natural death," she said, releasing herself from his embrace with a jolt and pushed him down on the sofa.

"How?"

"Poisoning," she suggested, taking off her panty, the only garment on her body. "Some road accident." She moved closer to him and unzipped his jeans. "Or some accident at home." She filled her mouth, taking off his underwear.

"Ahhh! Yeaaah! Accident at home…wo…would be…easy… something like suicide," he slurred in pleasure.

Ahi stumbled over those two names and re-read the para in disbelief; this fact was hard for her to accept. Her face distorted in disgust.

I was standing there by the door, witnessing the carnal journey of my son with my second wife. I have been watching them often, unbeknown to them. They cannot even think in their wildest dream that I can walk down to their room at night after Hari has returned to his outhouse.

I do not blame them for their physical relation though our society doesn't permit that between a stepson and a stepmother. Because they already had that relationship before I married Maya.

Dhruv had introduced me to Maya, a widow in her early ages as his girlfriend and he was willing to marry her. I had no problem with the relation, even though Maya is eight years older than him, until my network pointed out a few actualities of her past. According to my sources and their evidence, she and her parents had cheated several rich men after the death of her first husband. She lured them into the temptation of her attractiveness and made them marry her, just to take advantage of the law to accuse her husbands of domestic violence after few years of marriage. She is clever enough to manage huge alimony from each of her victims.

However, I had failed to make my son understand about her ugly face beneath the glossy skin as he is a slave of his own libido. Being compelled by those circumstances, I had to marry Maya to rescue my son. It did not demand much effort to buy her parents as some people are as saleable as vegetables. Initially, Maya refused to marry me, but later, she had to obey her parents. Moreover, the repetitive use of the same trick on their victims of domestic violence has become stale. So, they had to think of something different and big, which could settle their lives forever.

Now, I am the only obstacle in front of this cheap bitch as Dhruv can be manipulated easily after my death. However, she will not get anything even after my death, as I have already changed my will to donate all my property to an orphanage, cutting off Dhruv.

Tomorrow may turn out to be another judgment day of my life. Whether I will be the hunter or the prey, depends on the timing of the strike; I have to strike first.

Ahi flipped the page in the hurry, captivated by the story just to find the last page with two words,

The End

"Shit! What the fuck!" she screamed in frustration.

She kept the manuscript aside, got out of her bed, walked down to the window and lit a cigarette. The street in front of her apartment was lifelessly still. The beaming streetlights cast several shadows on the street. The closed tiny shops by the street and a cycle chained to one those lamp-posts, everything was motionless like a painting.

She kept staring at the shadows on the street finding their strange similarities with the manuscript. All the shadows hold the exact shape of its object, but never reveal the details of the object. She took a long puff and started exhaling the smoke slowly.

All of sudden, she felt as if the apportion of those shadows had moved. She leaned on her window to have a look at that portion. She rushed down the staircases to reach the ground floor and ran through the parking area to reach the street. She was panting as she reached the street. That silhouette was faintly revealing the details on the opposite side of the street; a person in a reddish saree. Ahi stepped forward to reach the other side of the street, but she stopped as her heartbeat raised, thumping on her rib cage. She was sweating in fear.

"Who are you?" she shouted from her place.

"You are not yet ready to face me," the silhouette replied in a male voice.

"Did you send me this manuscript and those messages on crumpled papers?" she asked in a low voice this time, as her heartbeats were slowing down gradually.

"Yes. And I want you to find yourself first. When you will do that, you will definitely come to know about me and a few other people around."

"Why me? Why can't you come forward and tell me directly whatever you want to say?" Ahi asked, throwing the cigarette butt into the nearest dustbin.

"You have to find all these answers by yourself and I will show you the path. Because you won't believe me if I tell you everything directly."

"Did you kill Devang and Dhruv?" she asked,

She did not get any reply as that six feet tall and hugely wide silhouette walked away. Ahi kept looking at it until it vanished into the darkness of the street.

Next day, Ahi woke up pretty late with an intolerable headache, but a missed call from Samim relieved her to some extent. She called him without wasting a second.

"Fuck you! What is this? Where have you been? Is everything fine, love?" she almost screamed as Samim received her call.

"Arey, there was some problem with my phone, so had to get it repaired. I am fine, nothing to worry," Samim lied.

"You should have asked for a spare mobile from them, right? How can you keep your mobile switched off for so many days, man?" She hollered not buying his excuse. Samim kept quiet. "Tell me, what's wrong? I know you Samim, you can't fool me," she asked firmly.

"Nothing Ahi. I think your new police friend has influenced you way too much to suspect everyone," Samim evaded the question, teasing her with a laugh.

"Oh yes! I have something to tell you about him but only after returning to Kolkata," she said softly.

"I am not sure when we can meet again."

"Why?"

"I am moving to Mumbai. I have got an offer for anchoring from a prominent and established channel," he informed.

"That's awesome! Congratulations!" Her voice has filled with excitement. "But you have rejected so many of them in the past. What's different about this? Why this change all of a sudden?" she enquired after a pause.

"Everyone is changing around me. It's only me who still believes those emotions and touches of childhood," he clarified and added after a pause, "Actually, I haven't changed, maybe just matured."

A silence conquered both of them but that silence was eloquent enough to express their emotions.

"When are you joining?" she asked, almost in a whisper.

"Tomorrow," he muttered in an inaudible voice, controlling his teary eyes.

"Okay! Best of luck then. I will definitely come to Mumbai to meet you sometime." More than him, she consoled herself. She wanted to request him to delay his journey for a few days, so she could meet him once before his departure. However, she refrained herself as it might sound selfish to him.

"Goodbye Ahi!" he whispered and disconnected the call before Ahi could respond.

Ahi comprehended his pain, but she did not have any consolation for him. She did not call him back, but left him to be healed by time.

❖

The repetitive thudding on the door broke Ahi's sleep; she got up, startled by the loud noise. It was dark everywhere in her room, except for a faint light that fell on the floor through the open window. She heard a few more thumping sounds on the door, their frequency and intensity increasing. She thought of changing her vest-top and shorts before opening the door but she felt too lazy. Moreover, that loud sound was unbearable. She stepped out of her bed, limped towards the door in a dizzy state and opened the door.

"Are you fine?" the silhouette at her door asked with intense concern in his voice.

She tried hard to identify that person but she failed as the bright light of the corridor behind him forced her to close her eyes. Anyway, she easily identified Abhimanyu's voice and responded, "Yes, why, what happened? Come inside."

"Oh god! I was so worried. I have been calling you since morning. Where is your phone?" he asked, leaving his shoes at the door.

"I don't know where it is, might be somewhere on the bed. Last night, I slept very late after finishing that manuscript. Then, that strange incident haunted me the entire night and I couldn't sleep soundly. Then, in the morning, Samim made me so upset that I was not willing to do anything but sleep," she said in a low, monotonous and sleepy voice, returning to her bed.

Abhimanyu was tempted to ask her about the 'strange incident' but he controlled his curiosity for the time being to cheer her up.

"Let's go out, enough of your sleeping in this dark room. It's almost six in the evening," he said pulling her up from the bed, holding her hand.

She sat on her bed reluctantly and whispered, "I might have lost him forever today."

"Who? Samim?" he asked to find the reference to her statement.

She nodded depressingly and said, "He is more than a friend to me. We have grown up together, sharing every minute detail of our lives with each other."

He sat on the bed by her and kept his palm on her as she continued, "I know why he is running away from Kolkata, but believe me, I have nothing to hold him back. I have never seen him like that and I can't even think of him like that."

She started weeping. He embraced her tightly and said, "Is it because of me?"

"No," she replied, hiding her face on his chest.

"Don't worry, he will understand you one day," he crooned, cuddling her face and neck and wrapped her within his tough and muscular arms.

"I am scared to lose everyone who has been a part of my life," she whispered, gently nibbling his ear.

"Then you don't consider me as a part of your life," he said softly, wiping her tears and took her lower lips in his mouth. She tightened her lips on his upper lip. She kept her lip locked in his mouth, unbuttoning his shirt. She moved his shirt away, rubbing her palms softly on his chest and tried to pull it off, holding the collar. But the tight grip of its sleeves on his muscular biceps defeated her. She giggled as he helped her take off his shirt. She pushed him down on the bed and started kissing that hard and ripped unevenness of his abdomen and that deep gap between the pectoral muscles of his chest. He closed his eyes, caressing her head. She started nibbling his biceps, forearms, chest and lower abdomen. She crawled down to his waist, opened his belt, unzipped his jeans and took it off. She kissed the edges of the twin curves over his pubic crest which narrowed down inside the wide strap of his underwear. He pulled her up, grasping her shoulders. He raised her on him slowly, with the help of his firm grip. He removed the straps of her vest top, letting it hang from her mounted breasts and pulled it down. He ran his fingers through her short hair, sharp jawline, scrawny neck, slender shoulders, soft breasts, flat abdomen and deep navel. She closed her eyes as goose pimples covered her. He raised himself on the bed, cupping her butt cheeks firmly. She tightened her thighs around his waist. She melted down on him, moaning as if she wished to wear him on her skin. She bit on his collar muscle sharply, leaving a mark.

"Ouch!" he screamed.

"Don't be dramatic. Otherwise I will chew you up completely," she whispered, slipping her hand inside his underwear.

"I… I don't have a condom," he muttered, fumbling.

"It's fine, just shut up," she said, pushing herself hard on him. She took off her shorts, stretched her legs.

"No way, I can't take the risk," he embraced her tightly to calm her down and kissed her on the forehead.

She shook him off to make herself free from his arms and said, "You are a spoil sport." She got down from the bed and put on her clothes.

"Come on! We can do it some other day when we are ready," he suggested.

"And If I die before that day?" she replied, lighting a cigarette.

"Don't talk rubbish, Ahi. Get me a cigarette," he almost shouted in irritation.

She lay back on the bed, resting her head on his chest and said, "Only this one is left," passing the cigarette to him.

"You know what… I feel like something terribly wrong is about to happen," she said in a low voice, abstractedly gazing at the open window. Before Abhimanyu could respond, she said, "Yesterday, I met that person who had sent me this manuscript and might have killed Devang Awasthi and maybe Dhruv as well. He was standing just a few feet away from me, wearing a red saree. We did talk and he walked away in that darkness."

"Praveen?" he asked.

"I couldn't see his face. But may have been a real transgender whom I met in that scrap dealer shop; the voice sounded familiar to me," she said quietly.

He smashed the half-burnt cigarette in the ashtray and embraced her tightly to comfort her.

"I am getting a weird notion that somehow, somewhere I am connected to all the crazy stuff happening around us," she almost whispered, creasing his forearm, brooding in her strange thoughts.

"Hey! Nothing to worry about. I know how strong you are. Don't you remember how you had protected yourself and Hari that night?" he encouraged her, kissing her on the forehead and asked, "Can I stay here tonight?"

"What's the point? Anyway, we don't have a condom?" she asked, staring at him.

"Not for that," he said, tapping on her head and laughed.

"His activities are teasing me as if he wants to challenge my capabilities. I hope he comes again tonight and… your protection also important to me," he clarified. Ahi nodded, kissing his face.

"Let's go somewhere; I am hungry," she proposed.

They freshened up and headed to a restaurant nearby for an early dinner.

Ahi shivered to step further into that endless darkness. She felt as if people were whispering close to her ears and she could sense their breathing on her skin. She swung her hands around to touch them, but her hands just cut through the air without touching anything.

"Who is that?" she screamed.

"You are not yet ready to face me," someone from the dark answered her.

She moved forward, groping on that wet, dirty wall which was covered with a layer of moss and saw a light falling on the floor. That faint light helped Ahi to understand the dimension of that gloomy place. She was walking through a narrow corridor which had a few rooms on both sides; few of them are closed and few are open, beaming faint light on the floor of that corridor. She walked down to that open door. One corpse was placed on a stretcher under a bright light hanging from the roof. That cadaver was covered with a white sheet. She entered the room tiptoeing and glancing all over the place around her. Her inner voice screamed, warning her to run, but her morbid curiosity was pushing her to explore further. She walked close to that stretcher and held the corner of that white sheet, hanging down from that stretcher. She quivered as a chilled wave passed through her spine while removing that sheet. She screamed, taking a few steps back, panting as she saw her own face, covered in blood. She felt someone's breathing on her shoulder. She turned back hastily to find a transgender who grasped her hand tightly, folding them to her back. She shook her hand to free herself.

"Leave me," she shouted, gathering all her strength and courage.

All of a sudden, she saw Abhimanyu in front of her, walking out from the dark corner of the room. She felt a soothing relief on seeing him. But he aimed his gun at her and pressed the trigger.

"No!" she screamed.

Abhimanyu woke up startled by her shout and rushed to the bed where she was sleeping.

"What happened? Bad dreams or something?" he asked, embracing her. She nodded, hiding her face in his chest.

After returning from the dinner, they hung out on the roof till midnight before Ahi hit the hay. Abhimanyu decided to stay awake, waiting at the window for that mysterious man. Ahi gave him company for a while, but could not hold her heavy eyelids open for long. Abhimanyu followed her after a few hours, dozing off on the chair in front of his watching-window.

"Have you seen anyone?" she asked softly in a sleepy voice.

"Not yet," he replied, sighing. "What was that dream about?" he asked, lifting her face from his chest.

"Some nonsense," she muttered, keeping her eyes closed as if she was scared to mislay her faith on him. She pushed his arms away slowly, making herself free from his grasp, and stepped out of the bed and walked towards the window.

"He is right there in the shadows of those trees, gazing at me," she whispered, watching the street after reaching the window.

"Where?" he asked impatiently, reaching the window.

"Shhhh! Don't shout and look for those blinkless eyes," she whispered.

Abhimanyu reached the door, running down the empty dining and drawing room, opened the locked door and started hopping down the staircase. He ran through the parking area, and reached the street. Initially, he could not see anyone on the street, but while glimpsing both sides of the street, he could see a shadow running. He started chasing the shadow. Abhimanyu could not see him very clearly as he reached close to him. He could not run as fast as Abhimanyu, as his saree was limiting his speed. Abhimanyu stretched his hand to grasp the extended part of his saree, but it slipped through his palm and he fell down on the street. The hard surface scraped the skin of his body at different places and made him realise that he was just in his underwear.

The man in the saree vanished somewhere while Abhimanyu stood up.

"He is not Praveen. But then, who the hell is he?" he muttered, clenching his teeth as he started returning to Ahi's flat.

He quickly put on his jeans and shirt after reaching Ahi's flat, instructed her to keep the door closed and drove away to the police station. Ahi requested him to wait till she applied an antiseptic from her first-aid kit. But he ignored her as his ego had much deeper, infected and painful wounds, than his skin.

That dream was still haunting Ahi. It was so vivid that she felt it had been a slice of her real life. That dripping blood on her face and that hatred in Abhimanyu's eyes while pointing the gun at her were terribly real. She could even feel the tactile recognition of a firm grasp on her wrists. It was really tough for her to get over it.

She stepped over something on the floor while she was returning to her bed. She switched on the light to find a brown envelope. She picked it up. There was a stone inside the envelope. She pulled out one of the two small pieces of papers from that envelope. The same typewriter had been used to print one line on the paper. However, its words knocked out her sense that time.

Doesn't that conch remind Pari of her brothers?

Her hand shivered while drawing out the other piece of paper from the envelope. It was a medium sized photograph of a family – A mother, holding an infant in her lap and two little boys standing by her. Ahi's eyes just glued on the eyes of that woman in the picture. They were sea-greenish, exactly like her.

She stood there in the middle of the room like a mannequin. She felt a strange heat under her ears and on the nostrils as she kept gazing at the picture and the chain of incidents rushed into her mind. The words of that transgender, *'Haye haye! Yeh toh saach main pari hai re'* rang in her ears. Then the words on that last piece of paper before in the envelope:

King's knight took Pari far away and gradually she became the universe of that knight.

She reminisced that day while her mother had explained the meaning of her name, Ahi.

"Sun, cloud, water, and earth... Ahi... the universe," she whispered. The conglomerated tears overflowed from the corner of her eyes and kissed her lips, rolling down on her cheeks.

"King's knight... Dhritiman Chatterjee," she muttered as her lips quivered, weeping. "Radha..." she mumbled, crying.

"What happened, sir?" Dubey asked as Abhimanyu stepped inside the police station.

"Where are Chaddha ji and Sharma ji?" he asked impatiently, rushing towards his cabin.

"I have called them as soon as you informed me. They must be on the way," Dubey replied, tagging along.

Abhimanyu nodded, considering it must be a tough call for those two middle-aged married men to attend an unplanned meeting at three in the morning. He hopped up on the table and gestured to Dubey to sit.

"What's the matter, sir?" Dubey enquired, failing to tolerate the suspense.

"Let them come, Dubey ji," Abhimanyu responded, playing with the paperweight on his table.

In the meanwhile, Sharma and Chaddha entered his cabin, almost running on their old feet. Abhimanyu gave them a few minutes to catch their breath.

"Within the next twenty-four hours, we have to arrest a transgender. I don't have any idea about his possible location, face or any other whereabouts. But we have to catch him," Abhimanyu declared, glancing over their clueless faces.

"How is that possible sir? They are huge in numbers within the NCR itself and as we are not sure about his location, he might be anywhere in India," Chaddha expressed his concern.

"I have already informed all the nearby bus stands, railway stations, airports and even all the check-posts on national highways. If he tries to get out of this city, he will be in my fist," Abhimanyu informed, toughening his jaw.

"It would have been tougher in the case of a man or woman. But a transgender, easily distinguishable anywhere, even in the most crowded area," Abhimanyu continued, walking around his cabin. "And we won't search randomly. Our every hunt should be triggered by our findings so far in this case. Haridwar, Ashiana, Awasthi Nivas and Awasthi Medical College and the hospital will be our triggering point," he added.

They nodded and left the cabin to instruct their team and all other unofficial networks around the city.

Ahi knew that time would not drift quickly if she kept looking at her watch repetitively. But she had nothing left in her life other than waiting outside that closed door of the front office of Ashiana. She simpered, thinking of the vulnerability and puniness of her life. A few words on a few pieces of paper and a photograph toppled her entire life upside down in a blink. But, she had to scrutinise them before being certain.

According to Devang Awasthi's manuscript, that honest investigating officer of Radha's suicide, had taken that infant to this orphanage, Ashiana. She had reached the place immediately after the first sun ray had fallen on earth that morning. She longed to talk to her parents, but she had been refraining herself to call them since the previous night.

All of a sudden, she heard the clang of that door behind her. She turned to find an old woman who entered that front office. She stood up and entered the room, following her.

"Good morning ma'am," she said in a low voice.

That old woman turned back, smiled, stretching the wrinkles over her face and said, "Morning."

"Ma'am, I need information of year 1992; whether someone called Dhritiman Chatterjee had adopted a girl child named Pari," she asked, trying hard to keep her voice steady.

"Oh! That's quite long ago. We might not have that on this computer," she informed, pointing an old computer on her desk and added, "I have to check that in the register copy."

She turned around to those gigantic metal shelves which covered almost all the walls of that room. After some minutes, she drew a thick and large register copy from one those shelves. She kept that on the table and started wiping out the dust on it with a piece of cloth.

"Generally, we don't entertain this kind of request until and unless we have an order from our managing board or police department," she informed wiping the register clean.

Ahi caught her gesture and put a note of five hundred rupees on the table. She picked it up in a hurry, smiled and said, "Please, don't take much time." Ahi nodded.

The register had many entries, divided into different months. Ahi flipped the pages and stopped on one page for the month of September, the month of her birth date. After riffling through a few pages, she stumbled on a row. That entry was made on a date which she knew as her date of birth till then. She re-read her parent's name in the same line just after the name, Pari. She kept her index finger under that line and read again, moving her finger through that row. Her vision blurred with tears as she reached the end of that line.

"Thank you," she whispered in an inaudible tone and left the room abruptly.

Ahi called her mother.

"Bahba! What's the matter? You remembered me, that too, so early in the morning," her mother mocked in good humour.

"Don't worry Maa. You will always be in my mind from today onwards, but might not be in my heart anymore," she replied in a steady voice.

Her words stunned her mother for a few moments before she asked, "What's wrong?"

"Can you put the phone on loudspeaker and call Baba as well? I have a question for both of you."

Her mother switched on the loudspeaker and called her father.

"We are listening, Ahi," her father responded.

"Why did you do this to me? How can you cheat me like this? You have always taught me to be honest and brave. You have raised me in a way to be a strong woman, independent in all aspects. Then why did you force me to live a life of lie?" she asked calmly, concealing her seething emotions.

"What are you talking about?" they asked almost in chorus.

"I know... I am your adopted daughter."

There was no response from her parents. "We...we didn't want to lose you, sona," her father replied, fumbling. That was the first time Ahi heard him being nervous.

"I am ashamed of that fact only, Baba. You guys don't even have this much confidence about me. That's the most hurting part. I know, I know the entire background of it and I don't blame you for that. But why did you lie to me?" Ahi's voice broke as tears gathered in her eyes.

"Sona, we are coming there. We need to discuss it," her Maa said, crying.

"Now? Don't you think it's too late?"

Ahi hung up bursting into tears while her parents were still trying to justify themselves. She knelt down on the ground, weeping. After a few minutes, she realised where she was and started walking out of that premises. She stopped suddenly as her eyes glued on a known face. It was not difficult for Ahi to identify the leader of that transgender group who rescued her in that scrap dealer's shop. His eyes were gazing at her.

Twenty hours had passed since Abhimanyu and his team started the hunt for that mysterious transgender. However, all their efforts had turned to naught. Moreover, the chances seemed most slender with the sunset. Abhimanyu was under tremendous pressure as his superior officer had already admonished him about resolving the murder cases at the earliest. The insistence of the circumstances got a sharpened edge that tested his patience while he had been failing repetitively to reach Ahi's switched off mobile since morning. Finally, he had to go to her place.

He pressed the door bell and waited for her response. After a few moments, Jaideep opened the door.

"Is Ahi at home?" Abhimanyu asked, impatiently.

"No," he replied, worried.

"Actually, I have been trying to reach her since morning, but her mobile is switched off. So, I was just wondering whether everything is fine," Abhimanyu said peeping into the flat over his shoulders.

"Please come inside. We might need your help."

Abhimanyu entered the flat. Jaideep took him to Ahi's room. The old man in that room, busy talking to someone on the phone, did not need any introduction. His eyes glittered in admiration, witnessing his idol, Dhritiman Chatterjee in front of his eyes. Abhimanyu guessed who the worried and perplexed woman on Ahi's bed was. She was in tears.

They had a lengthy discussion after Jaideep introduced Abhimanyu to Ahi's parents. Dhritiman gave Abhimanyu an update regarding their last conversation with Ahi. Abhimanyu was taken aback momentarily, learning the truth about Ahi's real parents. However, he recovered swiftly and that information comforted him in to some extent as he found some answers. Now they had to discover the identity of that culprit. According to all the information, Ahi was the only member of that family who was alive. Then, who was the transgender?

"Yes, Chaddha ji," Abhimanyu responded as soon as his mobile rang.

"Sir, his name is Munni. It was Munna in his childhood, but he changed that to Munni later," Chaddha informed excitedly.

"What else? This information is of no use."

"Hari brought him up like his own child after he started working in his restaurant in childhood. That's all we know about him as of now."

"So, we have a person who can get us the description of his face. Let's call our sketch-artist and get a sketch. I will join you soon," he instructed before hanging up.

Abhimanyu sat on the bed close to Ahi's mother and gently wiped the tears from her eyes. She gazed at his face with a blank expression.

"If there is anyone in this world who is the most worried about Ahi, after you and sir, that's me. I would like to die rather than return to you without her," he crooned, sandwiching her palm between his palms.

She exchanged a cold glance with her husband and nodded. Abhimanyu headed to the police station.

Ahi huddled on that tiny bed at the corner of that dingy room of a cheap hotel in Paharganj. That one lie shed all her beliefs, dignity and identity. The two people who she used to trust, respect, love and admire the most in her world, had cheated her. She was not ready to accept the fact that her entire life was a lie and based on an illusionary deception.

She grasped her cigarette packet. It was empty. She threw it against the opposite wall in frustration and screamed. Then, she broke down, crying inconsolably. Someone knocked the door.

"What the fuck you want? I don't believe you either. Please get the hell out of here!" she shrieked and started weeping again. She heard a few more knocks on the door.

"Leave me alone… please… please," she stammered, weeping.

Few more knocks on the door destroyed her patience. She jumped off the bed and rushed towards the door in anger.

"Why the hell have you been following me since morning? I think I made it clear to you that I am not interested in listening to your bullshit," she hollered, opening the door.

"I just want you to return to your family. It's my promise that you will never see my face again," the transgender said softly, with a smile.

"They are not my family anymore," Ahi shouted. Her face wrinkled in disgust as her voice empathetically whined that ruthless truth.

He laughed again and asked, "Do you mean that you trust whatever the bullshit I have written on those pieces of papers then? You believe that entry in the register of that orphanage, that picture and your resemblance with that lady in that picture?"

"Noooo," she screamed again, bursting into tears. "I don't know what to believe and what not. I just need some time and space to accept this brutal jest of my life," she mumbled, staring at that dirty fan that was struggling to spin.

"I just wanted you to know the truth of your life," the transgender said, clapping. He sat on the floor close to her and said, caressing her head, "You are an educated, independent, rational, brave and strong woman; don't disappoint my trust, Pari."

It was discomforting for Ahi to be addressed by a name she had learnt only a few hours ago. She stared at her face perplexedly as she had no argument to object. She was helpless to accept that new name which had crumbled all her age-long memories and existence.

"Who are you? How did you know about my tattoo? Why did you kill Devang Awasthi?" Ahi asked, gazing at his eyes.

"I will tell you everything, but only after dinner," he assured, placing a metal tiffin-box in front of her. "I know you have locked yourself in this room since morning. You must be hungry," he added, smiling affectionately.

She was so hungry that she jumped on the box, opened it hastily and started stuffing the food into her mouth.

"Slowly… slowly," he advised, guffawing.

It was half past eleven at night when the artist completed the sketch.

"He looks exactly like this," that witness almost shouted in excitement.

"Thanks for your cooperation," Chaddha said and asked him to leave. He arranged a vehicle for that sketch artist and returned to Abhimanyu's cabin.

Abhimanyu was carefully observing that sketch, as if he was trying to print that face in his mind. As soon as Chaddha entered the cabin, he threw that sketch in the air, letting it fall on the table and ordered, "Chaddha ji, circulate this sketch to all the police stations, bus stops, railway stations, check posts, hotels, shops and to all our unofficial networks in NCR."

Chaddha nodded and left, picking up that sketch from the table.

"He should not see the sunrise. No one can stop my promotion now," Abhimanyu whispered, lighting a cigarette.

Munni took out a pouch of bidis, confined under the strap of her bra beneath her blouse and lit one of them after carefully blowing both ends of it. He took a long puff from it and started talking, letting the smoke come out of his mouth and nose slothfully,

"I had grown up hearing my mother's cries and loud moans in pain from the other room of my home. I had seen my father send a different men every night to my mother's room in exchange for money. She was not able to speak, but her mesmerising eloquent eyes used to express her pain. She had the same pair of eyes like you."

"Is it you?" Ahi asked, pointing out the healthier boy among the two in that picture. Munni nodded, smiling shyly.

"And this is you," Munni said pointing the infant in that picture.

"Our father was evil. He used to consider Maa and me as his resources to earn money. He forced me to work in Hari chacha's restaurant when I was only six years old. At the end of every month, he used to meet me, just to snatch all my earnings. Bhai's retardation helped him to escape this rigorous imprisonment," Munni continued.

"So, I guessed correctly from that manuscript," Ahi commented.

Munni continued, "Thanks to god I met Hari uncle. He started helping me and Maa after comprehending our miserable situation. He even tried to get me admission in a school. But, my taboo puberty according to our society became an obstacle. Then the best possible incident happened in all of our lives – you were born."

Munni fondled her chin and kissed his own fingers. Ahi smiled, listening to his words.

"Maa seemed to get a reason to sustain her worthless and deplorable life. We needed more money to look after you. Maa started looking for a job to earn some extra money and got that opportunity to work in Awasthi Nivas. After few months, we came to know that our father was missing. We were happy as we never wanted to see his face again in our lives."

Munni paused, tearing some leaves of his childhood. As if he was visualizing all those incidents in front his eyes.

"I don't think you have read the manuscript. Otherwise, you would have known that Devang Awasthi killed him,"Ahi added.

"I know," Munni clarified, throwing the rest of his burnt-out bidi outside the window.

"Then why did you kill him? It was him who wiped out all curses from your life," Ahi asked curiously.

"I came to know about this manuscript after his murder. But, that doesn't make him innocent. I killed him for taking my mother away from me," Munni whispered, glowering.

"But she had committed suicide, right?" Ahi said, annoyed.

Munni replied, "She was forced to do that. Maa was very happy the day she learnt about the news of my missing father. She seemed to have gotten a pair of wings and decided to fly all over the city. She took us to several places, like the cinema, restaurant, park, zoo and many more. We all got a tattoo on our bodies to remember that day for the rest of our lives."

Munni lifted his saree along with the petticoat to show the conch, tattooed on his thigh and said, "I haven't seen yours, but I know, it must be similar to ours." Ahi nodded confirming.

"Then?"

"I was not working anymore. Hari uncle brought me many books and I loved to study. Our days were passing like some fairy tale. I was just about to return to Maa, bhai and you in Awasthi Nivas," he said with a pleasing smile on his face and took a pause, gazing at Ahi.

Ahi stared back at him with her impatiently curious eyes.

Munni's face contorted as she said, "But that bliss was washed away in a blink when I saw my mother, naked in Devang Awasthi's arms. I had decided to stay away from Maa as that incident bled my tender mind. That was the last time I saw her beautiful pair of eyes, but ashamed and hurt. After few weeks, I came to know about her and Bhai's death, but it was too late to find even their corpses."

Munni paused as tears overflowed his eyes. A suffocating silence spread across the room. Ahi wiped his tears, embraced his wide torso propping his head on her chest and whispered, "But they were happy to be together."

"You smell like Maa," Munni mumbled, crying. It took several moments for Munni to control his emotions.

"I was growing up with that one wish of my life – killing Devang Awasthi by any means."

"*Bol re,*" Chaddha said, responding to a call on his mobile.

"I have seen Munni near Paharganj railway station some hours back," the male voice responded.

"Stay there, we are coming," Chaddha instructed, hanging up the phone and rushed to Abhimanyu's cabin.

Abhimanyu jumped out of his chair, listening to the information and ordered, "Inform Paharganj police station to locate the exact place but not to take any action till we reach."

Chaddha nodded and rushed out of the cabin. Abhimanyu followed him. They started for Paharganj police station without wasting any more time at 1.30 a.m.

"So, publishing this manuscript was just an excuse to reach me and convince me of my real origin?" Ahi asked.

"That was one of the intentions. But the main intent was to defame Devang Awasthi," Munni said wiping the tears from his face.

"Why?"

"After I killed Devang Awasthi, I found him alive again in the mind of his million fans. That was quite frustrating for me as he was seen as a kind of hero. His existence was not restricted to his body. I had to wipe off the respect and admiration for him from peoples' minds," Munni explained, standing up.

"How did you come to know about me?"

"Dhritiman Chatterjee, that name was etched in my mind since my childhood. One day, I saw him on television when he was talking about the notorious rape case of Kolkata. I flew to Kolkata, just for confirmation, and came to know about your publication house. I never wanted you to know about this darkest side of your life," he continued, reaching close to that only open window of that room. Then turned back, rushed close to Ahi and holding her arms firmly, said, "Believe me, Pari. I had no other option but to involve you in this."

"I understand," Ahi said softly, resting her head on his chest.

"Can I have a bidi? I don't have any cigarettes," Ahi asked.

"Haye haye! Such a shameless girl you are. Didn't your parents teach you not to smoke?" Munni asked shockingly, pushing her away and covering his mouth with the extended part of his saree.

Ahi giggled and said, "Yes, they did."

"I can't spoil my sister. I won't give you one," Munni denied, making a sulky expression.

Ahi contorted her face, requested, "Only one… please."

Munni gave her a bidi and said, "Pari, promise me, behen, that you will return to your family tomorrow morning, publish this manuscript and forget about all this like a fictitious story."

"It's not possible for me to forget you as you are the only person who has a blood relation to me," she argued, lighting the bidi.

"What blood relation are you talking about? Whatever happened, happened for your good; otherwise your biological father would have sold you to some brothel. You are lucky to have perfect parents, people can only dream about. Moreover…"

Before Munni could finish his words, they heard a couple of knocks on the door. They muted, startled by that sound.

"Munni, open the door. We know you are here," a male voice shouted outside the door.

Ahi recognised Abhimanyu's voice.

"Police… quickly hide somewhere. I am opening the door," Ahi whispered.

"There is no place to hide in this small room," Munni retorted, pulling out a knife from her waist and held Ahi's throat from behind. Ahi stood in awe-stricken silence.

"Don't worry. It's just to fool your hero," she whispered with a soft laugh.

Ahi reluctantly comprehended his intention as they tiptoed towards the door together. The light knocks on the door had turned into violent and continuous banging. Ahi opened the door noiselessly and they took a few steps back. Abhimanyu entered the room opening the door with a hard push. Ahi's presence numbed him for a fraction of a second before he pointed his gun to them.

A strange felling nudged Ahi as if she was reliving that moment for the second time in her life. She became indifferent of her surroundings as her mind flew away to that room which she had seen in her dream.

"Munni, it's over! Leave her alone and surrender yourself," Abhimanyu roared like a lion, approaching closer to them. His alert troop was waiting outside the room.

"Your impotent law and order can't punish me more for an extra murder. My hand won't shake for a second to slit her throat and you will be responsible for that. Move away and ask your dogs to leave the door," Munni warned, stepping backward to the wall. Ahi got her senses back while Munni talked close to her ear.

Abhimanyu moved aside and ordered his men to allow them a way out. Munni got out of the room with Ahi and started walking back to the staircase.

"Pari, don't let this handsome go anywhere; he really loves you. I have to go…"

Before Munni could finish his words, Abhimanyu's gun wailed, emitting a tiny spark and smoke from the barrel. Ahi closed her eyes, startled by that loud sound and felt Munni's firm grasp on her chest loosening gradually. She turned her head to find Munni collapsing on the floor as Abhimanyu's bullet pierced her skull, right in the middle of her forehead.

Ahi stood there like a statue, gazing at Munni's lifeless body on the floor. The dripping blood from her head gradually made a cumulative puddle around her body. She could not hear anything around her other than an irritating resonation of that gunshot. She was blind beneath the layer of tears in her eyes. An intense grief cobwebbed and tangled her brain. She felt something heavy on her chest, strangling her breathing; she suffocated. She could feel her wild heart thumping on her rib cage wildly. She lethargically sat on the floor, placed Munni's head on her thigh, lifting it from the floor and started caressing her head.

"Ahi, are you fine?" Abhimanyu asked, placing her hand on her shoulder. She did not reply, kissed Munni's head and wrapped her corpse in her arms.

Few months passed after that incident. Ahi gradually recovered the trauma, evolving as a matured woman. She had created her own world which kept her busy in publishing work. Her parents were eagerly waiting for her wedding as they had no problem in accepting Abhimanyu as their son-in-law. However, Ahi requested them to allow her a few more years.

Abhimanyu reached Kolkata that morning as Ahi's parents had invited him to stay for a few days with them. He could not resist that temptation as it had been a long time since he had seen

Ahi. Moreover, Ahi had promised to show him every nook and cranny of Kolkata as it was his first visit.

Abhimanyu collected his bag from the conveyor belt and started walking towards the exit. His eyes were fiery and impatient, looking for Ahi in that crowd gathered outside that arrival gate. All of a sudden, his mobile vibrated.

"Yes sir. Thanks for your recommendation of my promotion," he greeted, picking up the phone.

"Our commitments are more precious than our lives and now you are one of us. We are quite impressed with your dedication and hard work," a male voice replied.

"Thank you, sir!"

"As a new member of the syndicate, we would like to give you a sensitive assignment which you have to accomplish to win our trust. You might have to break the law as well for this. Are you ready?"

"Yes sir, anything for the syndicate. I just want to see myself at the top," he reported firmly and waved his hand as he found Ahi in that crowd. He hurried to reach her.

"You don't have any other option as well. Once you are in, you have to obey all the decisions of the syndicate just for your own survival and prosperity," the voice paused for a moment and continued, "Devang Awasthi's Manuscript should not be published. It has ample information about the syndicate which we can't allow to reach the public. If needed, you might have to kill Ahi and all those people who have read it already."

Abhimanyu stumbled on his way to Ahi. She was approaching him, her face lighting up with that hypnotic smile which he could die for as her bluish-green eyes glittered in bliss.

***

Made in the USA
Columbia, SC
10 July 2023

20231611R00120